"I fantasiz~~e~~ ... female po~~liticians.~~

Holt moved from the doorway over to the bed, where Lacy lay sleeping. "But to find a redheaded mayor in my bed is the ultimate."

At the sound of Holt's voice, Lacy hopped off the bed and, half-asleep, groped for a logical explanation. "I didn't mean to do this," she mumbled.

"It's okay. I'll keep it quiet in the next campaign . . . for a reasonable payoff." Holt chuckled and lay on the bed. Even in her drowsy state Lacy was aware of his powerful masculine form sprawled across the covers.

"I guess I was more tired than I thought."

"Mmm. Helping a new employee move can be pretty grueling. Now how do you suppose I can thank you . . . ?" Holt smiled and pulled her down beside him. He kissed her deeply. "I can't believe I've just kissed the mayor," he murmured. "I hope I haven't breached protocol?"

Lacy felt a warmth spreading through her body. She had an overwhelming desire to kiss him back. "Of course not, Holt. The mayor *is* human." She moved her lips toward his. "Very human. . . ."

Mary Tate Engels has combined the real-life drama of several Arizona and New Mexico mining towns with the sizzle of romance to create her fourth delightful Temptation. Mary was fascinated by the fact that many of these struggling towns have lady mayors who are turning the economy around and creating a brighter future for their citizens. And Mary has added a touch of whimsy to *Best-Laid Plans* by giving the heroine an unusual hobby—cultivating herbs and edible flowers. But as for eating the flowers from her own garden, Mary says, "I haven't reached the point of munching on my pansies!"

Books by Mary Tate Engels

HARLEQUIN TEMPTATION
215–SPEAK TO THE WIND
243–THE RIGHT TIME

Writing as Corey Keaton
194–THE NESTING INSTINCT

Don't miss any of our special offers. Write to us at the following address for information on our newest releases.

Harlequin Reader Service
901 Fuhrmann Blvd., P.O. Box 1397, Buffalo, NY 14240
Canadian address: P.O. Box 603,
Fort Erie, Ont. L2A 5X3

Best-Laid Plans

MARY TATE ENGELS

Harlequin Books

TORONTO • NEW YORK • LONDON
AMSTERDAM • PARIS • SYDNEY • HAMBURG
STOCKHOLM • ATHENS • TOKYO • MILAN

To my three sons, Noel, Brent and Shane.
You are my inspiration, my resource, my reflections
and often, my entertainment.
Love ya' guys!

Published September 1989

ISBN 0-373-25367-2

1

"WE'RE GOING DOWN for the count, along with our town, if we don't do something." Mayor Lacy Donahue surveyed the committee of three gathered in her office.

"Any great ideas?" Sandy asked.

"That's why we're here." Lacy applied another floral garnish to the tray she was preparing. "To come up with some."

"I thought we were here for lunch," Annie said, slicing one of her famous apple cakes.

"I've heard of people talking to their flowers, Lacy, but you're the only one I know who eats them." Juvenile Judge Vinna Corona adjusted her glasses and peered skeptically at the array of colorful hors d'oeuvres.

"Think of them as edible garnishes." Lacy arranged another nasturtium on a cracker topped with cream cheese and passed the tray around. "Okay, now that lunch is served, the meeting's officially called to order. No, where's Maxine?"

"She can't make it today," said Sandy Amado, the high school math teacher. "She had a principal's meeting in Alamogordo. She asked us to keep her posted on the committee's decisions. I know she supports your efforts completely, Lacy, and that goes for all of us here."

Annie Clayton, owner of Annie's Apple Farm, nodded in agreement. "Right on! So, what are we going to do to save our town?"

Lacy smiled grimly at the small group. "I, for one, refuse to stand by and watch Silverton die. Not without a fight. I appreciate your support, and I need your input. Vinna, let's start with you."

"Never thought I'd say this, but your flowers are pretty good."

"Thanks." Lacy felt pleased that she had scored on one count. "Now, what about Silverton?"

"I see the results of the town's decline. Dropouts often end up in court, and I'm very concerned about our kids."

"But what about the jobless situation?" Sandy asked. "Doesn't that contribute to this rash of crime we seem to be having? There are only two places hiring—the prison and the junior college. Most of my students don't show college potential. That leaves the prison. The big question is, which side of the fence will they be on?"

"Sandy! You make it sound as though we're producing our own inmates!" Annie folded her arms on the table. "I knew that prison would cause problems here."

"Having the prison here isn't the problem." Lacy raised her voice above the clacking air conditioner. "Having limited opportunities for employment is."

"It's awful when families have to split up so both wage earners can be employed," Sandy added somberly.

Lacy nodded. "Everyone is suffering. We have a sick town, and it's up to us to make it well."

"Is it possible?" Annie adjusted her glasses and appealed to Lacy.

Lacy's gaze went to the courthouse window. In the school yard next door was a group of boys shooting baskets. They were happy and carefree, as youth should be. It only confirmed the importance of saving the town in Lacy's mind. "We're going to make it possible." She motioned for the committee to look outside. "For them."

Beyond the boys were the twin smokestacks of the now-empty copper processing plant. Those smokestacks had belched gray smoke until eighteen months ago, when the company had stopped production. The result was cleaner air in exchange for economic deprivation.

"For their sakes," Lacy said slowly, "and for ours."

Sandy reached for another flower-topped cracker. "You're right, Lacy. The kids are suffering most. We can't seem to keep good teachers. Our coach quit yesterday." She released a frustrated sigh. "Can't really blame him, though. He found a job in Albuquerque that offered him more money and the opportunity for advancement. He was our last male staff member."

They all nodded in silent agreement. Sandy's complaint was a familiar one. The coach, like everyone else, sought greener pastures, and Silverton's pastures were no longer green. They were more like dull brown.

Lacy rose to pour more iced tea for the committee. "I think we have to address the job market first."

Annie held her glass out for a refill. "But what can we do to bring more jobs to town?"

"What encouraged you to go into the apple business?" Lacy asked. "That's the spirit we have to tap."

"The apple trees need me," she answered simply. Annie's Apple Farm was struggling, which was one reason Lacy had chosen her for the committee. The other reason was that Annie was working hard to succeed. She had the spirit they all needed.

"No offense, Annie," Vinna said, "but a few good farmers won't solve our problems. We need more jobs than a couple of truck farms, even successful ones, can provide. I believe our young people are our greatest potential, but we have to keep them here or we'll lose Silverton's future, as well."

"Now Vinna, don't be so pessimistic," Lacy cautioned. "I realize choices are limited right now. But I still think Silverton has a lot to offer."

"What's wrong with that infernal air conditioner?" Sandy grimaced at the loud-clanking machine. "Is it working?"

"Barely." Lacy looked frustrated. "The shop can't get to it until next week."

"What we have is Vinna's pessimism and Lacy's idealism." Sandy fanned herself with her hand. "And lots of complaints. Meantime, the whole town's folding. Don't we have some realistic solutions around here?"

"Yes."

They all looked curiously at Lacy.

She pushed aside her lunch plate and leaned forward. "What if we developed a winning strategy, something to give the town a rallying point?"

"Like what?" Sandy propped her chin in her cupped palm.

Lacy's blue eyes lighted with a determined gleam, and she pushed back a strand of red hair. "What if we could do something with our town's own resources?"

"What resources?" Annie chuckled derisively. "Empty, run-down buildings?"

"Yeah. Special old buildings with an interesting, historic past and potential for the future." Lacy pulled copies of an official statement from her briefcase and passed them around.

Sandy skimmed the paper quickly. "Ah, I see the state funds came through."

"As you can tell from the figures, the amount's limited. But it's enough for a beginning." Lacy shrugged. "Now we have to decide the best use for this money."

"Are you thinking about renovating the historic section?" Vinna asked. "People have tossed that ball around for years."

Annie groaned. "'Historic'? You flatter those dilapidated buildings, Lacy. I thought you were coming up with a plan to raze that part of town and build a community swimming pool. Something fun if not useful."

"That'll come next," Lacy promised. "The community pool, not razing the buildings. Some of them are quite old, aren't they, Vinna? They have a history, a story to tell."

"Probably date back to the turn of the century, when silver actually was being mined here. Is that historic enough?"

"Should be." Lacy looked around and spoke slowly. "For an investment in Silverton's future."

"How do you figure this renovation as an investment in the future?" Annie countered.

"It's a potential tourist attraction. People love the old West."

"Make Silverton a tourist trap?" Annie scoffed. "Next thing you'll suggest is panning the creek for gold!"

"Not a 'trap.' A working replica. Buildings that function *and* provide historical information. Or whatever you think would be good uses for them. Businesses, archives, libraries, museums, theaters—anything!"

"We could probably get plenty of community support for renovating, especially from the old-timers," Sandy said with growing enthusiasm. "Many of them remember when the Mexican rebel Pancho Villa roamed these hills."

"I'll bet there would be plenty of folks who'd open businesses in those buildings if they were decent," Vinna said.

"I think so, too." Lacy fiddled with her plate. "Businesses will keep us going."

Sandy lifted her dark hair to get some air on her neck. "We'd have to hire someone to fix them up."

"Exactly." Lacy watched the group's reaction to each step of her proposal. "We have enough money to hire someone and to begin renovation. Meantime, we search for ways to attain more funds to finish the job."

"Sounds like you already have a strategy here, Lacy," Sandy commented.

The others began talking enthusiastically.

"Hold it!" Lacy raised her voice above the din. "Are we in agreement with this plan? Annie? What about you?"

"If you promise not to make it touristy. And if you think there are real profits for Silverton in the project."

"I definitely do." Lacy stood and gave the group a satisfied smile. "I'll admit we have a long way to go, but it's a start. A good one. Now, do I have your permission to hire someone for the renovation?"

"Yes, go ahead," the committee agreed in unison.

"I'll place the ad today," Lacy said.

As the committee filed out, Vinna stopped. "Two surprises today, Lacy. First your edible flowers and then the plan for the town. I'm learning not to underestimate you, Mayor Donahue. I think you might just pull it off. A 'winning strategy.' Not bad."

Lacy smiled hopefully. "Thanks, Vinna. I'm certainly going to give it my best shot."

HOLT HENDERSON FOUND it hard to believe that this narrow, twisting road was once a part of the famous Route 66 leading west across the country. The highway had been romanticized in movies, TV shows and songs. *"Get your kicks on Route 66."* There were no kicks on this grueling road now. The old highway had been bypassed for a more modern and direct route west, abandoning Silverton and other small towns along the way.

He didn't care. Silverton held potential. Silverton promised a future. Silverton was—he rounded a curve and his destination came into sight—a dusty, empty little town at the end of the road. He sighed. He'd hoped Silverton was the type of place he and Alita would like. Now he had doubts.

If it wasn't for her, he'd probably head for Oregon or Alaska. Someplace distant. But she was growing up and needed a stable home life. No more apartments and moving with every new job.

He and Alita had arrived early from Albuquerque to canvass the area and make their own evaluation. They found the city's business section limited, with many stores closed. The historical section was nestled against a low hill behind the courthouse. As expected, it was in ruins.

Silverton's quiet residential area was composed of once-beautiful stuccoed houses with turn-of-the-century gingerbread trim decorating the eaves and columned front porches. Most needed paint and repair. When they drove through the neighborhood, Holt noticed Alita staring curiously at the clusters of children playing in the neat little yards. "What do you think, honey?"

She returned his gaze with a hopeful smile that revealed two missing front teeth. "Are we going to live here, Daddy?"

"I have to find a job, first. That's why we came here today." Holt was glad Alita was a secure child who thought of life with Daddy as an adventure. She didn't remember her mother and didn't seem to miss having one. But Holt knew it was time to stay in one place. Alita would be starting school this year.

Holt drove back to the courthouse and parked on the nearly empty street. He surveyed the aging brick building as he helped Alita out of the Jeep.

"Forgot my coloring book!" She clambered back up into the seat.

"Got your crayons?"

"In my purse." She tucked the coloring book under her arm and tried to keep up with her father's long strides.

Holt paused momentarily, his attention diverted by two kids playing basketball on the school playground next door. The scene kindled memories of matching shots with his brothers when they were kids in El Paso. Those years seemed aeons ago.

One of the boys dribbled the basketball behind him, switching hands on the ball without missing a step. Then he moved around to approach the basket from the other side. With a graceful sweep of one arm, he dunked the ball then leaped high to recover the rebound. The other youth tried to defend the goal, but his swift-footed friend outmaneuvered him for another basket.

"Good shot!" Holt responded from the sidelines.

He chuckled and pressed forward again, his daughter in tow. He realized the presence of a six-year-old on a job interview wasn't very professional, but the sitter had gotten ill at the last minute.

"Can I stay and watch, Daddy?" She hung back, tugging on Holt's large hand.

"No, you'd better come with me. You can wait in the office while I talk to the mayor about a job."

"Then ice cream?"

"Sure, honey."

They stepped through warped double doors of the courthouse. The hallway smelled musty and old and was badly in need of some paint. The air wasn't much cooler than outside. Holt climbed the creaky stairs with Alita following and found the tiny, unimpressive sign that designated the mayor's office. Inside, a rickety air conditioner sputtered in one window, emitting a spritz of cool air and dripping a small stream of water beneath it into a pan.

Silverton's courthouse had definitely seen better days. Just like the rest of the town, Holt thought. Given Silverton's wobbly economy, seeking a job here might be risky. But it was a position he couldn't resist. Renovating a historic district was a rare opportunity.

Admittedly Silverton was struggling to make it. But so was he. Only time would tell whether either of them would come through. Meanwhile, the diehards could only hang on for dear life. Holt admired that kind of tough, western spirit. He considered himself of the same stock.

"Mr. Henderson?"

Jolted back to the moment, Holt turned around and gazed into the face of a lovely redhead with a pale complexion and a smattering of faint freckles across the bridge of her nose. She looked like someone who'd grab your hand and romp through a field of wildflowers. Holt stared at her for a moment, enjoying the fantasy. She smiled down at Alita, then turned her attention back to him.

"I'm Lacy Donahue." She extended her slender hand.

Holt blinked in surprise as he took her hand. "*Mayor* Lacy Donahue?"

"Yes."

"I hadn't expected . . ."

"I know. Someone so young. I've heard it a million times. But here I am. One and the same."

Her smile warmed him like the summer sun. He could smell her perfume, an unusual spicy fragrance that made him feel slightly heady. "It's just that a town like this—"

"A town like what?" Lacy withdrew her hand and gazed up at him. The color of her eyes reminded him of pale blue opals, delicate and rare.

"Well, it's so . . . historic."

She laughed. "You thought we'd all be antiques, like our buildings?"

"Something like that." Holt's gaze drifted over her casually ruffled red hair. She had a special energy, a clear spark of youth that was contagious. Yet there was a regal attitude about her that attested she was mayor.

Alita chose that moment to tug on Holt's sleeve. He looked down at the child with an expression that revealed he'd forgotten all about his daughter during this exchange with the lovely mayor.

"Daddy, can I go to the bathroom?"

Holt inhaled slowly. Back to reality. "Uh, I'm sure." He gave Lacy a weary look. "My daughter, Alita. Could she use your, uh—"

"Of course. My receptionist only works part-time. I'll show her." Lacy turned a gentle smile toward the child and stretched out her hand. "Come with me, Alita."

They started into her office, and Lacy looked back. "Why don't you come along, too, Mr. Henderson? Uh, into my office, that is."

He chuckled. "Sure." He followed as Alita chattered happily with the mayor.

"Are you going to give my daddy a job?"

"I don't know," Lacy said noncommittally. "We'll see."

"That's what my dad says when he's not going to do something."

"It's what adults say when they haven't decided yet." She opened a small door on the other side of her office. "Here. Do you need any help?"

"No, thank you."

"We'll be right out here." Lacy turned a smile to Holt and motioned for him to sit. "She's charming."

"Talks too much." Holt had learned his lesson about bringing Alita along. Never again. He sat opposite the mayor and watched Lacy with pure pleasure on his face.

Everything about this woman was warm and amiable. The mayor carried herself straight and proudly, even though she dressed modestly in a cotton blouse and skirt. Her alluringly spicy fragrance negated the old-building smell in her office. She seemed to radiate energy through the room.

Lacy settled at her desk and opened Holt Henderson's application. Of the three applicants she'd interviewed, this man was the best qualified for the job. His experience in remodeling was extensive, and his background in architectural history was a definite plus for their needs.

It hadn't escaped her notice that he was rather handsome—dark hair, a rugged, sturdy build. He was the kind of man who would look just as impressive in a pair of work jeans and a T-shirt as he did in the navy blazer and tan slacks he'd worn for the interview. There were so few men around town, she'd forgotten the nice feeling of a man whose masculine appeal could dominate a room. And as softhearted as it seemed, Lacy didn't mind that he'd brought along his little girl. It showed a tender side to the man.

She gazed up at him and smiled. "I've reviewed your résumé, Mr. Henderson, and I'm impressed."

He nodded a brief, modest thanks.

"Tell me about your historical projects."

"I worked in Florida, Georgia and California for several years after college. We were a small organization, hired specifically for historic renovations. As you might imagine, work was sporadic, and we had to travel to jobs. Eventually, the group fell apart as various members married and settled down. I tried to continue alone, but with the latest market slump, it's been impossible. Now I'd like to start fresh."

"I can understand." Lacy, of all people, could certainly understand starting fresh.

The bathroom door opened and Alita emerged. With the innocence of a child, she walked to her father and leaned on one of his legs. "How much longer, Daddy?"

"I think you should wait in the other room, Alita."

"We'll leave the door open so you can see your daddy." Lacy indicated the chair opposite the door. "We won't be very long. I see you have your coloring book. Good."

Alita followed Lacy into the outer office.

"We won't be long, Alita," Lacy repeated. "Then we'll all take a walk."

Alita's expression brightened, and she crawled up into the chair. Holt wondered miserably if he could lose a job because of one little girl. She seemed to be demanding so much attention.

Lacy smiled gently at Holt as she took her seat at the desk again. She sensed his discomfort. "I don't mind having her along. Really."

He shifted in his seat. "I . . . my sitter got sick this morning. I had no alternative but to bring Alita along."

Lacy noted that his magnificent gray-blue eyes, while revealing strength of character, also showed signs of stress. She glanced back down at the résumé before her. "Marital status: Widowed." So he took care of his daughter alone? Before she could ask, he explained.

"Her mother died in a car accident five years ago," he continued, sensing an explanation was needed. "And I have full responsibility for her care. She's the main reason I'm here. It's time we settled down. Alita starts school this year."

"So, if the job works out, you plan to move here?"

"Absolutely."

"I'm sorry to hear about your wife, Mr. Henderson. It helps to know that you have a real interest in living in Silverton." Lacy wondered briefly if she should be completely honest with him about the risks of the job. She decided to wait.

He shrugged. "I'm basically a family man with a child to care for. That's most important to me right now."

Another plus, she thought. Unwittingly Lacy found herself accumulating reasons for hiring him. Some of the reasons had less to do with his work skills and more to do with just plain liking him. He had an easy style that made him appealing. She envisioned the committee—the whole town, in fact—responding positively to Holt Henderson.

"Why did you apply here?" she probed. "Do you know the gravity of our town's economic situation?"

"Almost everyone in the state's aware of your problems. Frankly, the historic aspects of the job interest me."

"What do you think about the future of Silverton now that our major industry has pulled out? Does that concern you?"

Holt folded one leg so that his ankle rested on the opposite knee. One large hand circled the ankle. "Sure. I'd be lying if I told you it didn't. But, given its potential, this town should be able to survive. I'd like to be a part of that, especially if it's related to the renovation of a historical section."

"Do you really believe we can make it?"

"From what I've read and seen today, Silverton is still viable. It's a pleasant place to live, with a good climate and relatively good farmland in the valley. The mountains are close, and apparently a substantial number of people want to work and live here. That speaks well of a place. I expect some innovative industry will look closely at Silverton's assets, including a built-in work force. Already you have the junior college and the prison."

"Funny you should mention our work force when so many have left town looking for jobs."

"That should be your number one priority, then."

Lacy leaned forward with a little grin. "If this job doesn't pan out, would you consider working for our Chamber of Commerce, Mr. Henderson?"

He shrugged. "It's just an observation."

"And a good one. It corresponds with mine. I'm very optimistic about our future. Do you have any questions about the job?"

"I'd like to evaluate the buildings and see how much work is needed, what you want done and what your time schedule is."

"That's next." She folded his application. "Our first step was to find someone who could do the job and who was interested in sticking with it until completion. You sound as if you're willing."

"Willing and able."

Very able, she thought, trying not to show her admiration of his physical condition. Lacy placed her palms on her desk and pushed herself up. "Shall we tour the district? Your daughter can come along with us."

"Sure." He waited while she preceded him, and he caught another whiff of her spicy fragrance. Her femininity was asserted in that glorious, exotic aroma, and Holt decided that following Her Honor had definite advantages.

He took Alita's hand, and they walked out the rear door of the old courthouse. A grass-infested, broken-brick sidewalk led to the time-ravaged historic section. Vague remnants of patios existed among the weeds, bricks crumbled from slanting walls and paint chipped from weathered gray boards. The whole place was terribly run-down, and the casual observer would have declared the area a disaster. But not Holt.

Lacy didn't try to hide her dismay. "Some people around here have recommended that we raze this area and install a community swimming pool. They feel it's more trouble than it's worth to fix up."

"I think that would be a major mistake." Holt moved ahead of Lacy, caught up in the experience of examining the various structures. "It would be a real tragedy."

"Why do you think so?" She hurried to keep up with him.

"Just look!" He made a sweeping gesture. "Where are you going to find such diversity in historic design? Right here we have Sonoran adobe, mission revival, Anglo territorial, even a columned Greek revival."

Lacy was impressed with his knowledge but more interested in his enthusiasm. She paused in front of the Greek revival building. "This was a bank. They say Pancho Villa and his gang of revolutionaries hid out here one night."

"And next morning they had a shoot-out with federal marshals." Holt finished the story with more details than she knew. "Miraculously they escaped into the mountains, and the marshals left the county empty-handed. The band returned a week later, on their way to Mexico, and kidnapped one of the local maidens. She never returned."

"I'm impressed."

"History major, remember." His expression was animated. "Silverton has a vivid history that should be preserved. And it's up to us . . ." He halted. "Er, up to you to preserve it."

As they continued the tour, Lacy felt growing admiration for Holt Henderson's ability to see Silverton's potential. "Our goals are simple," she said. "We'd like to start from scratch, renovating one building at a time. The ideal situation would be to get one completely finished and functioning so the town and the government agencies can see our purpose. In order to get their help, I think it's important to show them that the project is viable."

"Sounds like a reasonable plan." His expression revealed the confidence she wanted to see.

"We want to create a lively town again. It's that simple." She lifted her chin. "And that tough."

"I can do it," Holt said confidently.

"You can?" Lacy studied him. She liked his positive attitude. It stopped short of being arrogant but indicated a strong self-confidence. She took a deep breath. "Mr. Henderson, the people around here haven't had much experience winning lately. I'm afraid they've forgotten what it's like."

"I hope you aren't fooling yourself about how hard you'll have to work to turn this town around." He looked at her steadily.

"Not at all. We're anticipating—hoping—the renovation program will give everyone a rallying point and encourage their participation."

"That's quite a challenge."

"Would you be willing to participate with local organizations who want to contribute to the project? For instance, if a group wants to donate a Saturday, would you supervise their work?"

"Sure." He watched his daughter hopscotching on a worn spot near an overgrown central courtyard and ambled toward her. "Are you saying I'd be in this project alone, except for the volunteer groups?"

"At first, yes. But you'd be in charge. And responsible." Lacy followed him. "You know, lots of our kids' fathers have already left town looking for work somewhere else."

"And you want to bring them back?"

She nodded. "For more than the weekends."

"Maybe you're striving for the impossible."

"Nothing's impossible."

"Sounds like you expect miracles."

"I guess we do need a few miracles." Lacy brushed a golden-flame curl off her forehead and gazed up at him with a stout thrust of her chin. "So what's wrong with that?" She was tallying her evaluation of Holt Henderson. Was he the one capable of creating miracles for them?

"I only believe in miracles when they're preceded by hard work." He stuffed both hands in his trouser pockets and let his gaze roam the grounds. "I'll bet this area would be perfect for an old-fashioned gazebo."

"A gazebo?" She squinted in the direction he was looking, and her imagination began to work on the idea he'd proposed so lightly. "Yes, a gazebo. With wandering sidewalks and scattered flower gardens. This could be a lovely park, a gathering place for families. Picnics and a Sunday afternoon band and a theater-in-the-round for summer nights. . . ."

He turned and walked slowly back to her with a little-boy grin. "I'd like to see that, Mayor. To see if there are any miracles left in this fine old town."

"So would I." Lacy was flooded with the certain knowledge that Holt Henderson was the man they needed. He had revealed insight toward Silverton's requirements as well as an understanding of the challenges. He knew it wouldn't be easy. She was convinced that he wanted to see it happen, just as the local townspeople did. What's more, he wanted to lead the project. That's who they needed. Someone with vision as well as ability. "Shall we go back to my office, Mr. Henderson?"

Lacy had a strange theory. When there were big decisions to be made, she humored the situation with food or drink. It seemed to make the effort more palatable. There was no food in her office, but she often brought a large thermos of her own blended herb tea. She went to that thermos as soon as they walked through the door. "Would you and Alita like some iced tea?"

"Yes, thank you."

Lacy dug out three plastic glasses. Standing with her back to her guests, she carefully prepared the drinks. Ice from a small Styrofoam ice chest, a sprig of mint, a twist of lemon and then the amber-colored tea. To the child's, she added sweetener. By the time she finished, Lacy had made her decision. She set the glasses before Holt and his daughter. "Mr. Henderson, I'm prepared at this time to offer you the job."

"It . . . it's mine? You're sure?"

"If you want it."

He gazed curiously at her for a moment, nodding slowly. He pressed his lips together and glanced down at his daughter, then looked away and lifted the glass of tea to his lips. The moment was conspicuously quiet except for the sound of his swallowing.

"You can take some time to decide and let me know," Lacy said to fill in the silence.

"No. I don't need more time. I came here to get this job, and if you're offering, I'll take it."

"Great," she said with a sigh of relief. She extended her hand to him. "I think we're very lucky to have someone like you on our team. You have the kind of expertise and energy we're looking for, Mr. Henderson."

He rose and took her hand. "I'll do a good job for you."

His attitude was confident. She liked that. "There are some papers for you to sign, but you can wait until you report for work. Is two weeks enough time for you to take care of your business in Albuquerque?"

"Yes. That's fine. And thank you, Mayor Donahue."

"Please, call me Lacy. We're very informal around here."

"Right. And I'm Holt."

Lacy smiled happily. She was pleased with her choice. And she felt certain the committee would be, too. "I suppose you'll be needing to find a place to stay. Our chamber has a complete listing of available homes. It's on West Third."

"Thanks, I do. We may as well take care of that while we're here."

"Are we going to stay this time, Daddy?"

"Looks that way."

"Long enough for me to have a puppy?"

"We'll see," Holt said.

Alita faked a slap to her forehead. "Oh no! Here we go again!"

They all laughed at her antics, and Holt decided it might not have been such a bad idea to bring his daughter, after all.

A little later, Lacy stood at the front office window, watching the two of them stroll down the sidewalk. It was particularly heartwarming the way the tall, lean man protectively clutched the small girl's hand. She detected a strong bond of trust between the child and her father, which spoke well of the man she'd just hired.

Lacy returned to her desk to tackle the unending stack of paperwork. What a relief to have found someone so qualified and experienced. She could hardly wait to report to the committee. One item accomplished, she mused, on the long road to success.

Scarcely a minute later, her office door swung open. Startled, Lacy lifted her head to face the man she'd just hired.

"Call the police!" he demanded. "My Jeep's been stolen!"

2

"I'M SURE there's been some mistake."

"Somebody *mistakenly* drove off in my Jeep?" Holt's gray eyes swept over her desk. "Where's the phone? I'm gonna—"

"H-hold on a minute." Lacy stood, her mind racing. She certainly didn't want to culminate this interview with a call to Sheriff Meyer. "Let's check this out first."

Something about Lacy's expression caught Holt's attention. She was showing sufficient alarm at his announcement, but her beautiful blue eyes grew intense and seemed to beg for restraint. Her body stiffened, and one hand reached out as if to halt him from further action. Maybe she was the type who froze in an emergency.

Their gazes locked. His was puzzled. Hers, questioning. Obviously she was hoping he'd remember that his car was actually parked on the other side of the building.

"No, I didn't forget where I parked it," he said in answer to her silent plea. "What else do you want to check out?"

"Well, uh..." Lacy's thoughts tumbled wildly but only one lingered. Do something to stall and maybe the situation would improve. "Details. Tell me exactly what happened."

He glared at her, thinking that every second allowed someone to get farther away in his vehicle. His lips thinned as he spoke deliberately. "I parked it in front of this building about an hour ago, and when I returned, it was gone. Zip. *Nada.* Tire tracks in the dust leading—" he paused to gesture dramatically "—into the sunset."

"Exactly where did you park?" She moved from behind the desk and toward the window that held the dripping air conditioner. "Show me."

He hovered close behind her, trying to avoid the moisture-spitting spray from the machine as he pointed to the street. "Right out there, in front of the oleander hedge, beyond the hoop where two teenage boys were playing basketball. As you can see, neither boys nor Jeep are there now. And we did arrive in a wheeled vehicle. Need proof?" He rattled a set of keys in front of her nose. "I have these, which means someone wisely hot-wired it. Something teens are prone to do if they're bored on a hot summer day."

"Don't jump to conclusions, Holt." Lacy's heart sank and her mouth grew dry. It was sounding worse, not better! "Give me the description," she managed, thinking that she would have to call the police, after all.

"An '81 Jeep, silver and black. Because of its age, only insured for liability, not collision or theft. So if it's stolen, it's gone. Tough. I'm out of wheels and outta luck." He shrugged, then turned to pace the office. He had to get away from her. It was hard to be angry standing so close to her. "But, I can describe the two kids who were playing basketball. One was tall and blond, the other was dark and tough looking."

"He could play basketball real good," piped Alita, who'd been quietly standing beside her father. "And he could jump real high."

Lacy swallowed hard. She was almost sure the blond he referred to was her friend Sandy Amado's young brother-in-law, Steve. Basketball was his favorite sport and she saw him almost every day in the playground practicing shots. Surely he wouldn't get involved in car theft, though! Holt must be mistaken.

He faced her in a defiant stance with feet wide apart and arms folded across his chest. "Are you going to *do* something?"

"Please find our Jeep," Alita added with a little whine to her voice.

Holt, usually so tolerant of Alita's verbiage, wished she would hush. Bringing her wasn't so smart, after all.

Lacy glanced distractedly at the sweet-faced child, who folded her arms to mimic her father. There was no sympathy in her gray eyes, either.

"Look, I hate to accuse those kids." Holt propped his fists on his hips, and suppressed anger began to show in his narrowed eyes. The motion made his shoulders look even broader, his expression even more fierce. "But you've got to admit, it doesn't look good for them."

Lacy nodded miserably. "You're right. I just wish we could get to the bottom of this without involving the sheriff." But there seemed no alternative. After all, the man's vehicle was nowhere in sight, and chances were, his observations had merit.

At that moment, someone knocked twice on the office door and entered without waiting for an answer. "Is this the mayor's office?"

"Yes." Lacy gaped at the woman dressed in a pink pullover, jeans and high-topped work boots. Low on her hips dangled a leather belt, from which hung several hand tools.

"I'm here to check on the air conditioner."

"Now?" Lacy snapped. "Great timing."

The woman angled her hip prominently and propped one hand on it. "Don't tell me you're that way, too."

"What way?" Lacy tried to tear her thoughts away from Holt's missing Jeep and the tense situation at hand.

"You probably think I can't fix this machine because I'm a woman."

"Me? Oh, no, that's not it at all. It's just that— Oh, never mind. I'm sure you can repair it." Lacy backed away from the spewing air conditioner, giving the street one last glance.

She gasped aloud at what rolled into view. A black-and-silver Jeep! Intact! She practically jumped up and down. "There—here! Is this it, Holt?"

He lunged back to the window and muttered an expletive. "Joyriders! I'll show them—" With one long stride, he was out the door, his woodsy fragrance lingering in the air.

"Nice looker," the repairwoman remarked.

Alita raced after him and Lacy gestured futilely at the air conditioner. "Check it out. I'll be right back." She dashed after the other two.

They converged on the Jeep as it pulled to a stop. "Oh no!" Lacy groaned when she recognized Steve in the passenger seat. She didn't know the kid who was driving. He must be new in town.

"Get out of there!" Holt demanded, jerking on the door handle.

Both boys tumbled out, and Steve mumbled immediately, "Sorry Mayor Donahue."

"I just can't believe this, Steve."

The boy shuffled and kept his eyes to the ground.

The other kid spoke up. "We didn't mean nothin', man—"

"Who are you?" Lacy asked.

"I'm Roman Barros. Look, I didn't mean no harm."

"Any harm," Lacy corrected.

The dark-eyed kid nodded. "Right. We thought we could take a little spin before you got back. No big deal."

"No big deal?" Holt folded his arms across his broad chest and glared ominously at the two. "What gives you the right to take a little spin in my Jeep?"

"Hey, man. We jes' did it."

"We intended to bring it back all along," Steve explained. "Before you got back."

"You can't just get in other people's vehicles and drive around," Lacy implored.

"That's called stealing," Holt advised, his expression grim. "Wonder what your folks would say about this. Or the local police."

The boys looked up at him in alarm, and both spoke at once. "Oh no, please don't do that!"

Holt's expression changed from tight-faced anger to calculated manipulation. They'd given the reaction he sought.

At first, Lacy feared Holt might still press charges. He had every right. For the boys' sakes, she reverted to a more formal way of addressing him. "Please, Mr. Henderson, let's talk this over and, uh, settle it some other way."

He turned to her. "Don't tell me you're one of those who coddles offenders of the law. Well, I think people should be responsible for their acts. Don't you agree?"

"Yes, of course."

He turned to the boys. "Don't you?" He paused and both boys nodded in agreement. He continued. "I don't appreciate you fellows taking advantage of those of us who abide by the law. If you'd wrecked the Jeep, I could have lost my only vehicle. I don't have insurance to cover it. Do you?"

They shook their heads. Obviously "insurance" was a foreign word to the kids.

Holt continued, gesturing. "What if you fellows had been injured! You'd be in the hospital right now, and your families would certainly be notified then."

The boys looked whipped.

"Could we work out some kind of deal?" Lacy began to recognize Holt's tactics and hoped he was sincere. A court appearance over this wouldn't help any of them, and the kids might end up in juvenile detention in Alamogordo. "Since I know Steve and his family, don't you think we can do something about this without calling the authorities?"

Holt braced his chin with one fist and considered her proposal. "I don't know. They need to learn a lesson here."

"I'm willing to supervise some instructional punishment," Lacy offered. Her gaze lingered on Steve. "Your brother would be so disappointed, Steve."

"Please don't tell Jay, Ms Donahue," Steve mumbled, keeping his gaze on his toes. "He'd be furious."

"Look, dudes, it . . . it was my idea," Roman admitted when he could see Lacy's attention centering on Steve. "I hot-wired it, and Steve just went along for the ride. We thought sure we could get back before you came out."

"Thank you for admitting your part in this, Roman. But both of you are guilty, and both of you must pay."

She turned to Holt. "I think Mrs. Novak, our high school principal, said her office needed a fresh coat of paint. What if these boys volunteered to do it, Mr. Henderson? Would you be satisfied with some hard work?"

Holt pursed his lips for a few agonizing moments. Finally he nodded slowly. "Well, that might be enough punishment."

She rushed ahead. "I'll see that they pay for your inconvenience and bother, Mr. Henderson. They'll regret this little spin in your Jeep, I promise. And I think I can assure you, it'll never happen again. Will it?"

"No, sir," both boys mumbled at the same time, shaking their heads and looking to Holt for approval of the idea. "It won't."

He studied each youth with a steady, penetrating gaze.

"Fortunately no one was harmed, and you do have your Jeep back." Lacy gazed up at him hopefully. "I'm sure they took it without thinking of the consequences."

Holt sighed. "I guess you have a point. It would serve no good purpose to drag the police into it now. But boys—" he paused to point a finger at each of them "—if anything like this happens again, you can bet that I'll show no mercy."

The boys, looking numb, nodded mutely. Right now, they probably would have agreed with anything he said if he'd just drop it and leave.

"Thank you, Mr. Henderson," Lacy said, shaking his hand and indicating for the boys to do the same.

Holt gripped each boy's hand firmly, letting them know full well his strength. Then he helped Alita into the Jeep and walked around to the driver's side. "I'll be in touch," he said tightly to Lacy, who'd walked with him. "See you in two weeks."

"Thanks for the reprieve. They'll remember this close call." She waved and he drove away. Then she folded her arms, tapped her foot and glared hard at the boys. *Now* she could show her anger. "You two got off easy, you know that?"

"Yes, ma'am," Steve mumbled. "Thanks for helping us out of a jam. You won't tell Sandy and Jay, will you, Mayor Donahue?"

Lacy shook her head. Should she? Sandy deserved to know when the boy was in trouble. On the other hand, Jay was working out of town, leaving Sandy responsible for Steve. This news would only add to her pressure. Anyway, Lacy felt that she had the situation under control. "No, I won't tell her about this, Steve, but I want your promise to stay out of any more trouble. And you . . ." She turned to the other boy. "Have you recently moved into town?"

"I live out that way." Roman gestured to the west.

"Do you have family here?"

"Uh, just my aunt."

Lacy observed that Roman's eyes shifted as he spoke, and she tucked the information away. "Will you be going to school here, Roman?"

"Yeah, probably."

"How old are you?"

"Sixteen."

"Then I expect you to enroll in high school next week and to attend regularly. I'm going to check on you."

"Yes ma'am."

"I have an idea." Lacy smiled grimly. "There's another chore you two might do to make up for this little joyride. Mr. Henderson will be moving to town in a couple of weeks. He could always use some strong guys to help move his furniture."

"Yeah, we could do that," Steve said, nodding.

"A cinch," Roman added. "Does this mean that we don't have to paint that room you were talking about?"

"No," she said firmly, giving them each a narrow-eyed glare. "Report to the school office at eight in the morning. And you're still getting off light." She wheeled around and returned to her office.

Hot, stuffy air greeted her. The repairwoman, down on her knees in front of the silent air conditioner, gave a low groan. "Bad news."

"What now?"

"I think this air conditioner has taken its last gasp."

"So what's new?" Lacy moaned and appealed to the ceiling. "What else around this place is going to go wrong?"

"I'm afraid it just isn't worth it to repair the thing." The woman gathered her assortment of tools and began to stuff them into her belt.

Lacy sighed heavily. There was no money in the budget for an air conditioner right now. "Well, summer's almost over. We'll just have to manage without it."

The woman looked at Lacy curiously. "Are you the new lady mayor I've heard about?"

"I'm the mayor, all right. What have you heard?"

"That you're tough and smart. And if anybody can bail this town out of its mess, you can."

Lacy straightened and pushed an errant curl back. "I'll take that as a compliment. After this day, I need one. Yes, I intend to keep this town going. Which is more than I can say for this air conditioner."

"Good luck. Since I couldn't fix the thing, I won't charge for this service call. You—and the city of Silverton—look like you could use a little break."

"Thanks." Lacy gave the repairwoman a grateful smile and shook her hand. "I, er . . . we need all the breaks we can get."

When she was alone again, Lacy glared at the offensive and now-silent air conditioner. She was overwhelmed with the urge to punch the damned thing, just to relieve her frustrations. Instead, she raised the window above it in an effort to get some air stirring. A less than cool breeze ruffled her red hair.

With a resigned sigh, Lacy turned back to her cluttered desk. So she'd found the perfect man for their winning strategy, hired him, and the first thing the town kids did was offend him by joyriding in his Jeep. What if he reconsidered and backed out of their deal?

Finding a replacement for Holt Henderson would not be easy. There hadn't been many applicants and none with his excellent credentials. Plus, he'd behaved admirably today, considering how angry he was when he'd first reported his vehicle missing. He was right. It *was* serious. But he'd taken the whole thing like a gentleman and surprised her with his tactics for dealing with the boys. Surprised, but also pleased her.

Holt was a very capable man. He didn't shirk from his tremendous responsibility of single parenting, and she admired that. Yet no one could blame him if he declined what small security Silverton had to offer.

Lacy slumped in her chair. *Oh please, don't let us down now*, she begged silently. *Don't quit. We need you, Holt Henderson.*

3

HOLT HENDERSON wasn't a quitter. His determination was too strong to be deterred by a couple of thrill-seeking kids.

Having grown up in a houseful of boys, he understood their fascination with motor vehicles and their thrill-seeking adventures, which occasionally included flirting with the law. He figured the incident was handled and closed. And he didn't plan on seeing those kids again anytime soon.

On a sunny Saturday two weeks later, he pulled a U-Haul truck to a stop in front of the quaint, Queen Anne-style house he'd rented in Silverton. His hands rested on the steering wheel for a moment as he gazed at their new home . . . a new beginning.

The house, a historian's delight, featured a gabled window surrounded by fish-scale shingles. Some of those decorative shingles applied to the front facade were missing, and one of the windows was cracked. The front porch was supported by turned columns and topped with a row of knob dowels. Like everything else in this town, the house needed repair and paint.

"Come on, Daddy! Let's go inside!" Alita pushed on Holt's shoulder, and he slowly obliged. She explored the porch while he unlocked the door. Then she burst through the house with all her six-year-old energy.

Holt stood in the entrance hall, trying to absorb the place. Twelve-foot ceilings, wood-paneled doors with ornate hardware and wide plank floors meant that, in its day, the small home had been quite attractive. It had potential.

The two bedrooms, living room and kitchen were built around a central structure containing the bath, bedroom closets and the kitchen pantry. Holt sighed. At least it wasn't an apartment. They'd have privacy and a feeling of settling down in a real home.

He'd been enthusiastic about the move until now. So why was he feeling reluctant and pensive today? Doubt? Facing the unknown? No, he wouldn't let those feelings dominate. He was probably just tired and needed to finish this last step. Whatever the reason, he tried to shake off the mood without much success.

"Come on, Daddy! Let's see if they left the swings in my backyard!" Alita bubbled with the eagerness he lacked. She was already possessive. *My* yard.

Holt moved through the old-fashioned kitchen, ignoring its inadequacies. Right now all he cared about was that the refrigerator and stove worked and the sink had hot running water. The backyard was fenced, barren of all but a few clumps of grass, and so small that the child's A-frame swing set practically filled it.

"My swings!" Alita squealed with delight as she pumped her short legs. "Look how high I can go, Daddy!"

He stared bleakly at the space with its sandy, naked spots in the grass. It wasn't beautiful, but maybe with a little work and water, he could make it homey. It was better than apartment dwelling, where they had no privacy. As he watched her, Holt couldn't resist giving Alita a fatherly warning. "Be careful, honey. Not too high...."

"Daddy, please!" She admonished him, then hopped down and grabbed his hand. "Let's get our stuff out of the truck. Come on, I'll show you which room is mine!"

He followed her back inside. "I think both bedrooms are about the same size."

"But I want this one so I can look out my window and see my puppy in my backyard."

"What puppy?"

"Daddy! *The* puppy!"

"I think we should clean this place up before we start hauling stuff inside. We'll discuss the puppy later." He turned in the hall and came abruptly face-to-face with Lacy Donahue.

She smiled, a little chagrined at having walked in uninvited, a little overwhelmed at the sight of him. Just as she'd suspected, he *was* an eye-boggling hunk in a sleeveless T-shirt and faded blue jeans. "Your, uh, door was open, and I, uh . . ." she began weakly. "Welcome to Silverton, Holt. Did I hear you mention cleaning?" She smiled and pulled a mop into view. "I just happen to have some equipment with me."

"Well, hi." He was caught off guard and gaped at her dumbfoundedly. With her flaming hair pulled into a ponytail and a few wispy curls teasing her ears, she looked like a teenager instead of the town mayor. She wore a sleeveless, oversize shirt belted over jeans that were rolled to her calves. Sloppy socks fell over high-topped tennis shoes.

Suddenly, for absolutely no reason he could pinpoint, Holt's sagging spirits melted away, and he was glad to be here today. He was especially pleased to see Her Honor. "Lacy, nice to have you here. But I'm surprised. Does the mayor offer her cleaning services to everyone who moves into town?"

"We have so few folks moving in, it's really a big deal. I thought about hiring a band." Lacy propped both forearms on the mop handle and grinned teasingly, hoping she was hiding her private admiration. The man exuded an overwhelming masculinity, with his broad shoulders and muscular arms, trim waist, narrow hips and long legs. She sucked in her breath and tried to get a grip on herself. "I, uh, when you gave me your address, I knew we lived close. So I watched for your moving truck."

"You live near here?"

"Just up the street. The house on the corner."

"Oh. Small world, huh?"

"Small town. No one lives far from anyone else." She nodded past him. "What do you think about the house? Will everything fit?"

"Oh yes. I don't have much." He motioned. "Take a look around. It needs a good scrubbing and a coat of paint."

"I'm surprised you'd notice. Most men wouldn't." Lacy knew instinctively that Holt Henderson wasn't like most men. She gave the house a quick once-over and ended up in the bedroom that Alita had claimed. "Hi. Is this your room?"

"Um-hum." The little girl stood by the window, looking out. "Isn't it nice and big?"

"It's very nice. Do you remember meeting me?"

"Sure. You're the mayor. Did you come here today to visit us?"

"Not exactly. I'm here to help you and your dad move in."

"Goody. I think we're going to need it," Alita said with childish honesty. "This place is pretty dusty."

"I even brought my own mop and rubber gloves."

Alita motioned out the window. "I have a backyard for my puppy. And a swing. Would you like to see how it works?"

"I'd love to." Lacy propped her mop by the door and, accompanying Alita, gave Holt a cheerful smile as she breezed past him.

Holt realized he'd been standing in the hall, watching Lacy interact with his daughter. The unorthodox mayor was a colorful, lively whirl of energy, who, even in casual garb, was quite attractive. He could hardly take his eyes off her. Wheeling around, he headed outside to the truck—his original destination before Lacy Donahue had spun into his day. He didn't even notice that he was whistling now.

As he dug into the back of the U-Haul for assorted cleaning equipment, a compact car pulled to the curb across the street. A young woman and teenager hopped out and approached him. Holt recognized the kid as one of the boys who'd taken the joyride in his Jeep.

The smiling woman extended her hand. "Hi. I'm Sandy Amado. You must be Holt Henderson. We've been looking forward to your arrival."

"Nice to meet you, Sandy."

"And this is my brother-in-law, Steve."

Holt's gaze met Steve's as they shook hands, and he realized that Sandy didn't know about the joyriding incident. Her friendliness was too naive. "Steve, Sandy... a pleasure."

"Steve says he was asked to help you move in," Sandy said.

"Oh, uh . . ." Holt gave Steve a puzzled look.

"Mayor Donahue asked me and Roman to come over today," Steve said quickly. His expression practically begged Holt not to question why. "Roman should be here soon."

"Oh. Well, we have plenty of work for everyone." Holt motioned to the house. "The mayor is already here. We're going to start by cleaning."

"I'll leave you fellows at that," Sandy said with a chuckle. "I have my own housecleaning to do today. Nice to meet you, Mr. Henderson. We're glad to have you in Silverton." She turned to Steve. "I'm going to visit Mama, and we'll see you later. Now, don't be late for supper. Jay'll be here, you know."

"I'll be there on time." Steve waved as Sandy headed for the little pink adobe house across the street.

"Well," Holt began. "Nice of you fellows to give up your Saturday for me. You take this, and I'll get the rest." He shoved a bag of sponges and a broom into Steve's hands, then rummaged in the truck for more.

Within a couple of minutes, Roman arrived on a little motorbike, accompanied by a blare of rock music. "Yo, man. Need some muscles?" Roman headed toward Holt, a large "boom box" balanced on his shoulder.

"Hello, Roman." Holt extended his hand for a firm handshake. "Nice to see you again. Before the muscles, I need some elbow grease."

"Say what?"

Holt chuckled and lifted a box of Spic and Span. "Cleaning power. Elbow grease. Then the muscles to move the furniture."

"Oh. Sure, man." Roman shifted from one foot to the other.

"Come on. Steve's already here, waiting for you. And I need to have a little talk with the mayor." Holt strode inside and approached Lacy, a curious expression on his face. "Looks like the gang's arrived. Real friendly town. Everyone's turning out to help me move. Would you like to let me know what's going on here?"

Lacy forced a smile. Her cheeks flushed, and she motioned him into the kitchen. "I should have discussed this with you earlier, but there wasn't time." She knew that wasn't *exactly* the truth. Her attention had been captured by Holt and his little daughter, and she'd temporarily forgotten Steve and Roman.

"How many more are coming?"

"No more. Just these two." Her blue eyes widened as she hurried to explain. "I hope this is okay with you, Holt. It seemed the best way to discipline them. You see, neither of the boys wanted their little excursion revealed to their families, so I decided they should work directly for you in exchange for a little discretion."

"I see." Holt pursed his lips. "This is your plan, I take it?"

She nodded.

"And that's why you're here?" He'd wanted to think she was there just for him.

"To make sure everything went okay," she confirmed. "And to help you, Holt." Was she really there to make sure the boys behaved? Or had she used that as an excuse to get to know more about Mr. Henderson? Lacy wouldn't second-guess her own intentions at this point.

He assessed her for a moment, his gray eyes turning to steel. "Well then, we may as well get busy." He started to turn.

She caught his arm. "You aren't angry with me, are you? I thought it would help."

"Help who? Me or the boys?"

She shrugged. "Both. They work. You benefit."

He paused, his renewed spirit suddenly deflated. "I just like to know what's going on, Lacy. And now I do."

"And you don't approve." Her fingers continued to clutch his sinewy forearm. "Maybe it's a big mistake. We could all leave. Or . . . I could go."

"No." His gaze met hers. "Please stay. It's okay. I just . . . Never mind."

"All right." She released his arm, unable to shake the feelings that surged through her when they touched.

Without another word, he turned and joined the boys, who were standing in the hall joking. "Why don't you guys start in the living room? Here's a bucket."

Lacy stared after him. Her decision to recruit the boys had seemed so simple in the beginning. But now . . .

For the next few hours, conversation was sparse as everyone scrubbed the little house from top to bottom, keeping time with the throbbing rhythms from Roman's "boom box." Even little Alita did a six-year-old's share, usually working by Lacy's side. Holt supervised the furniture moving, and when the truck was empty, Lacy volunteered to bring over pizzas and Cokes. Twenty minutes later, she placed them on the table.

Alita peered inside one box. "What's the green stuff?"

"Zucchini," Lacy said grandly, opening the other box and inhaling.

"What are those black things?" Steve wrinkled his nose.

"Hey dude, olives!" Roman answered.

"Zucchini?" Alita's voice was small and intense. "And olives?"

The three kids looked at one another, and Lacy knew she'd flubbed. "Lots of cheese, guys. Real good for you."

Their expressions said they didn't care.

Holt stepped forward and took a large slice of the zucchini one. "Thanks, Mayor. This looks great. One of my favorites. Try it, guys." He took a bite and chewed while they watched. When the bite was gone, he grinned and winked at Alita. "You can't even taste the green stuff."

Roman shuffled closer to the table. "Hey, I like olives." He picked up a slice of the olive pizza and took a bite. "This one's better 'n most."

Reluctantly, Alita and Steve each took slices. After a moment of silent chewing, they nodded. It was a slow beginning, but the group eventually devoured all but two little slices. Lacy figured it was only because they were practically starving.

When they had finished eating, she noticed Roman gazing longingly at the remaining pieces. "Would you like more, Roman? Please help yourself."

He looked up quickly, surprised that she could read his mind. "Well, I, uh . . ."

"Go ahead," Holt insisted, shoving the flat box toward him. "We've had it. If you can hold more, help yourself."

"Uh, not for me. But if you don't mind, uh, I'd like to take it home to my sister. She's like—" he paused to nod toward Alita "—like that little one."

"You have a sister at home?" Lacy closed the box and handed it to Roman. "Well, of course. Take both pieces—one for your aunt, too."

"Aunt? Oh, yes. Uh, thanks."

When the boys left, Lacy began cleaning up the kitchen. Holt leaned against the cabinet and finished his Coke. Alita wandered into her bedroom, and soon they could hear her talking softly to her dolls.

"I'm sorry I brought the kids here without consulting you, Holt." Lacy spoke with her back to him as she finished wiping the table. "But, you see, the boys need so much. And I was hoping, that is, well . . ."

"It's okay, Lacy."

She turned around to face him. "No, I want to explain. This town's in trouble. And so are our kids." Her voice lowered. "Maybe all of us are. I felt that the boys' taking your Jeep was a call for help. And I didn't think a call to the sheriff would be the kind of help they needed. They were reaching out, and I, as mayor, happen to be in a position to make an attempt to help in a positive way."

"It was a good plan. The boys helped a lot today. And I assume they learned their lesson not to mess with the mayor."

"Or her employees," Lacy said with a snap. "Sandy Amado, the woman you met earlier, is a good friend. She's trying so hard to keep track of Steve. Jay, her husband, is working in Santa Fe and only comes home on weekends. They would have a fit if they knew Steve got into any kind of trouble like . . . like stealing your Jeep."

"Trying to keep family harmony, huh? And Roman? What's his story?"

"I don't know him. Only that he lives with an aunt outside of town. Today I learned he has a little sister. But I'd almost bet he's in some kind of trouble."

"You think he needs a break, too?"

She nodded and lifted her chin. "We all need a break around here, Holt. The town of Silverton needs a break, and I figured you were the one to give it to us. Guess I—" she paused "—figured wrong."

"Wait a minute. You think that my remodeling the historic section is going to do it?" He shifted from one foot to the other. "Come on, Lacy. What's really behind this? Discipline for the kids or—"

"I told you." She looked away, then quickly returned her gaze to his, fire in her eyes. "Okay, okay, here goes. From the beginning, I liked you. I felt you were the right man for this job, Holt. You're the kind of man we need around here. Strong and self-assured and hardworking. But when the kids took off in your Jeep, I was afraid you'd back out and leave us flat. When you didn't, I respected that. Today I wanted everything to go smoothly." She shrugged. "So the way to make sure was by being here."

"You want everything to go smoothly to make sure I hang around?" He gaped at her skeptically.

She nodded silently, feeling manipulative and miserable.

To her surprise, his face broke into a slow grin and he leaned forward. "I have no plans to leave Silverton. I have a job here, a job I want very much. And my child is expecting to live here. I can't continue to uproot her at my whim. Unfortunately, there's no guarantee that what I do will keep this job going—or save this town, Lacy."

"Yes, it will! I'm convinced it will, if we all work together. We'll make it happen."

Holt gazed at her for a moment. Her enthusiasm had suddenly flourished into a bright radiance in her blue eyes. And it made him think he could make a difference.

Just then Alita appeared in the doorway and announced, "I'm going to play in my backyard."

"Sure, honey. Have fun," Holt responded absently, not taking his eyes off Lacy. She was full of delightful surprises, and he was still trying to figure her out. And figure out his own responses to her.

Alita skipped away, and for a moment, the adults completely ignored her. But when the screen door slammed, Holt looked up and called, "Be careful on those swings, Alita. Not too high." He looked back apologetically at Lacy. "I have to work to keep from being a hovering father."

"You're doing fine. Better than I did with the vegetable pizzas." Lacy wiped a crumb she'd missed from the table. "Guess I struck out with them, huh?"

"They ate every bite."

"They were starved." She grinned. "I should have known better."

"Are you one of those vegetarians?"

"No, not strictly. Since sausage and pepperoni aren't high on the nutrition list, I thought I'd give them some different choices."

He leaned on the refrigerator and laughed. "But zucchini and black olive—"

"I learned my lesson." She raised her hands, palms out. "Never again. Next time, I'll take a consensus. . . . If there *is* a next time."

"I'd like that—a next time." He nodded toward the table, now cleared of pizza remains. "Have a seat."

"Thanks, but since you're all moved in and everything went smoothly, I'd better be going."

"Don't. Not yet."

She looked up at him, curious.

"We haven't really had a chance for privacy...to talk. If we're going to be working together, maybe we should

get to know each other." He gestured toward a chair.
"Sit down and split this last Coke with me."

"Well, okay." She took a seat and realized how tired
she was. Sitting felt fabulous.

"Since you were so honest with me, I'll confess
something I hadn't planned on telling." He opened a
Coke can, poured its contents over ice in Styrofoam
cups and placed one in front of her. "Not yet, anyway."

"What's that?"

"From the first I liked you, too."

Lacy almost choked on the drink. "Huh?"

"It may even have influenced my decision to take this
job." Holt walked to the window to check on his
daughter. "Along with the nearly perfect small town,
terrific job, and of course, the private backyard for Alita." He ambled back to the table and sat opposite her.

"Don't forget the ease with which we helped you
move in." Lacy grinned and took a sip of Coke.

"I'll need even more help. Maybe you know of a reliable sitter for Alita."

"I could probably give you a few names."

Their conversation began to flow effortlessly. Holt
felt Lacy's warmth, her friendliness. He responded
positively to her and liked being with her. Her upbeat
attitude had been contagious today, both to him and to
the kids. The man in him found her attractive and sexy,
even dressed in that overlarge shirt and rolled up jeans.
Unglamorous, no airs and honest. She was a natural
beauty who needed no makeup and had the most fabulous eyes he'd seen this side of the movie screen.

"What are you doing here in this one-horse town,
Lacy?"

"After my divorce, I came to Silverton to start over."
Her blue eyes crinkled warmly at the corners when she

smiled. "I grew up in a little town near here that has since folded completely. I decided I didn't want that to happen to Silverton."

"How long have you been here?"

"Four years."

"And you were married . . ."

"Five years."

"No kids?"

It was a natural question, yet it always ripped at her insides. "No. So it was uncomplicated. He settled. I left town."

"And where was that?"

"Fort Worth, Texas."

"How did you get to be mayor here?"

She gratefully moved on to a happier subject. "I have a political science degree and have always been interested in local government." She paused, thinking how Jason resented the county council meetings she used to attend in Fort Worth. "When I arrived, Silverton was already on a downhill slide. The incumbent mayor had been in office a hundred years, or so it seemed. Nice guy, but no new ideas."

"And, of course, you had ideas."

"Barrels of them!" She chuckled. "I campaigned on the promise that we would pull ourselves out of this financial slump by our bootstraps. It was just what the people around here wanted to hear. I was very optimistic then. Maybe 'idealistic' is a better term."

"And now?" He gazed at her with a gleam of admiration in his gray eyes.

"Well, I'm not idealistic anymore, although some think so. I'm still optimistic, but now it's mingled with a healthy dose of realism. I'm out of a job if the town goes under."

"Me, too. I need to settle down, for Alita's sake. She needs better security, a homey atmosphere, a backyard. Maybe even a puppy. Those things are important to a kid. And I intend to provide them for mine." His lips formed a determined line. "So you see, Lacy, I need this town, too. Maybe as much as Silverton needs me. I have no intention of leaving—"

The moment was shattered by loud wails coming from the backyard.

"Alita!" Holt surged to his feet, noisily overturning his chair in the process.

Lacy scrambled after him. By the time she arrived on the back porch, Holt was cradling his small daughter in his arms, a look of terror on his ashen face. "I think she's hurt bad. Look how she's holding her arm."

Lacy moved closer and slipped two fingers against Alita's palm. Instinctively, the child squeezed. Lacy rubbed the top of the small, soft hand with her thumb. She looked into Holt's frightened eyes. "I don't think her arm's broken. Just to be sure, maybe we should take her to get an X ray."

"Oh my God—"

Lacy slid her other hand to Holt's sinewy arm and pressed reassuringly. "It'll be okay, Holt. Accidents happen to kids. And parents fix them up again. That's part of being a parent—" Her voice caught in her throat. Who was she to tell this capable father anything about parenthood? Through tight lips, she muttered, "I . . . I'll get my car."

4

"THE DOCTOR SAYS it's pretty common for kids to get a broken clavicle."

Holt gazed at Lacy wearily. The skin around his eyes showed signs of the stress he'd been under for the past couple of hours. "Yeah. Common for rowdy boys of ten. Not for little girls of six."

"So she's rowdy." Lacy smiled sympathetically at the dozing child in Holt's arms. The shot the nurse had given Alita was already taking effect. "She's advanced for her age. And being a modern girl, she doesn't adhere to the old stereotypes for girls and boys."

"Great." He rolled his eyes. "Then I have all the boy stuff to worry about as well as the girl stuff?"

"Well, you're a modern father. You can handle it."

"Not very well when it comes to my little girl, apparently." He stroked the small, limp hand resting on his chest.

The touch evoked a wellspring of emotions inside Lacy's heart, and she caught her lower lip between her teeth. That simple act of affection showed the devotion the man had for his child. And the way Alita clung to and now slept on her father revealed her solid trust in him.

It was a beautiful moment, one that Lacy cherished. And one she'd never have. But she had reckoned with that long ago. Tonight she kept her facade intact, careful not to expose her true feelings.

Holt's strong gray-blue eyes softened. "I don't know what I would have done if you hadn't been here, Lacy. You kept your cool when I was too upset to think straight, and I appreciate it. Thanks, Mayor."

She shrugged and pushed aside her emotions. Pretending was her specialty now. "What's a mayor for, if not to help out a little?"

"This'll make a great campaign story when you run for mayor next term."

"I have to prove myself this time around first. Then I'll consider another term. The townsfolk may think I don't deserve one."

"They'd be fools to let you go."

"If Silverton isn't on its feet three years down the road, or headed that way—" She made a cutting sign across her throat but halted when the nurse returned with a prescription for Alita.

Holt listened to instructions on how to take care of his injured child for the next few days. Then Lacy drove them back home. While Holt tucked Alita into bed, Lacy scrounged in a couple of boxes for a pan and some instant coffee and fixed them each a cup.

"Kids are amazingly resilient, aren't they?" Holt walked into the kitchen, looking somewhat relieved for the first time in several hours.

Lacy gazed at him with a warm smile. She couldn't help admiring the inherent strength of the man who'd held his little girl so tenderly during her period of trauma. Now, although his calm was completely restored, she knew him to be vulnerable in some ways. Still wearing the same jeans and sleeveless T-shirt, he dominated the small space of the old-fashioned kitchen. He seemed invincible.

But Lacy knew better. Actually, he was a man in need of comfort and solace. In that moment, she wanted to be the one to give it. She wanted to wrap her arms around him and say, "There, there, it's over. Your child's okay. You did exactly the right things." She wanted to caress his brow and press his head to her breast. She wanted to kiss away the pain.

Instead, she motioned jerkily to the table. "Have a seat. Here's some coffee to tide you over for the trip."

He heaved his long body down in the ladder-back chair. "Thanks. How'd you find anything in this mess?"

"I dug around in a few boxes. Hope you don't mind."

"Not at all." He ran his hand over his face, then looked back at her. "What trip?"

She sat opposite him and propped her elbows on the table. "Don't you have to get that rental truck back to Albuquerque tonight?"

He shrugged and took a sip of coffee. "Hey, it's late."

"If you don't get it back tonight, you'll have to pay for an additional day," she added pointedly.

"You've used this method of moving before, huh?"

"Several times," she said, momentarily recalling the most recent and worst one, when she drove herself to Silverton after her divorce. It was so hard to admit defeat and start over at square one.

"But Alita's asleep and—"

"I'll stay with Alita."

He looked quizzically at her. "No, it's too much to ask. You came over for a couple hours of cleaning and moving, and it's turned into an all-day-and-into-the-night ordeal."

"You aren't asking. I'm offering." She folded her arms on the table and kept her expression serious. "No, as your boss, I'm telling you."

He quirked one eyebrow. "The mayor can be a little domineering."

"How do you think I got to be mayor?"

He grinned. "Pure guts."

"I'll tell you about 'pure guts' sometime, Mr. Henderson. But right now—" Lacy straightened in her chair and gave him a demanding look "—would you quit chatting, drink your coffee and get on your way?" She shoved him away with her hands. "Go on now."

He took a quick, deep breath. Then he gazed at the open doorway into Alita's room. "You sure?"

"Positive. She'll be fine. After that shot they gave her, she'll probably sleep the whole time and never know you're gone."

"Okay. I'll be back as soon as possible."

"Don't go over any speed limits," she warned as he headed for the door. "That's where I draw the line on helping."

He gave her a mock salute and disappeared into the darkness.

Lacy sat with both arms stretched out on the table on either side of her cup and listened to the truck roar away. She took a deep breath and let it out slowly. Then another.

She was tired, too. But the worried expression in Holt's eyes this evening as they'd waited in the emergency room for the results of Alita's X rays had prompted her to want to do more.

Maybe it was a desire to make things right for this man she'd just hired. Strange, she barely knew Holt Henderson, yet she felt as if he were an old friend. He seemed to fit in right away. He was the kind of solid citizen that Silverton needed.

She finished her coffee and washed their cups in the sink. Then she ambled through the house, stopping in Alita's doorway to observe the sleeping child for a moment. The ruffled pink curtains in the little girl's room lent a tiny feminine touch to the rather heavily masculine household.

Holt's furniture was a lot like the man. Sparse and rugged. It revealed his admiration for history and southwestern design. Some of the pieces were quite old and stylish, and she wondered about this man who collected antique furniture and worked on antique buildings.

In the living room, a low pigskin table with a mesquite-slat base served as a coffee table. A sturdy sofa with an oak frame was piled high with many colorful pillows. Two barrel chairs with calico cushions flanked the front window. A table lamp with a carved wooden base sat on a rough-hewn table between them. In the corner, a rocker made of saguaro ribs looked so inviting that Lacy took a seat.

For all of its crude design, the chair was actually comfortable, and she leaned her head back and rocked. She wondered where Holt got the chair and if he ever sat here. It had a large seating area and probably fit Holt's long frame better than hers.

Lacy thought of how Holt Henderson's acceptance of this job had changed everyone's outlook. He had given Silverton an added boost of optimism. She'd always maintained hope for the town, but Holt added a missing ingredient. Confidence. There was something special about him that drew her to him. Perhaps it was his motherless child. But she couldn't deny the physical attraction that she had felt immediately for him. She'd just have to be aware and watch herself.

As Lacy sat staring out the window into the black night, she noticed a light in the Carson house across the street. Mrs. Carson, Sandy Amado's widowed mother, was an affectionate lady who didn't hide her disappointment that Sandy hadn't produced any grandchildren for her in four years of marriage.

Lacy felt a pang in the pit of her stomach. The memories were too real. She knew that kind of pressure—and it was awful. Oh, Mrs. Carson meant well. She wanted to dote on someone, and her desire to have grandchildren was natural. But while Lacy took the occasional hints to heart, Sandy laughed them off, saying, "If Mama had to face a roomful of squirming kids every day in the classroom like I do, she'd cool it."

The real reason the Amados hadn't started a family was economic and, Lacy felt, tied directly to the poor job situation in Silverton. Also, Sandy and Jay had assumed the responsibility for his younger teenage brother, Steve. It was a tremendous financial burden for a young couple, one of whom had to travel out of town for a decent job.

Maybe if Mrs. Carson had more to do—Lacy sat upright and snapped her fingers. She might be the perfect sitter for Alita. The responsibility would give her a child to dote on, someone who needed the attention. Then maybe she'd stop pressuring Sandy to have a baby.

Lacy heard an unfamiliar noise and listened intently for a second. Then she recognized the sound of a child whimpering and went immediately to Alita's room. Murmuring low, soothing sounds, she adjusted the soft harnesslike brace that held Alita's shoulders back and kept her clavicle immobile until healing could take place.

"Where's my daddy?" Alita whined sleepily.

"He's gone to take the moving truck back. I'll be here with you until he returns."

"Oh." Alita paused, then added, "I'm thirsty."

"I'll get you a drink." Lacy brought her a Styrofoam cup of water.

"Daddy went back to our old house?" Alita asked between sips.

"He had to get your Jeep. But he'll be back here tonight." Lacy smoothed the child's forehead, then kissed it. "When you wake up in the morning, your daddy will be here. And you'll feel better."

"Okay...." Alita settled down on her pillow and soon drifted back to sleep.

Lacy tiptoed from the room feeling very motherly, but relieved that Alita wasn't upset to find her father temporarily absent. She was, as Holt had said, pretty resilient.

Lacy paused beside the open doorway to the other bedroom, the one that Holt would use. The bed was unmade, boxes were stacked in front of the closet, and a small draftsman's table occupied the corner. Nothing in the room was arranged, and she thought of him returning in a few hours, tired and needing a place to sleep. Without thinking further, she began opening boxes.

Shortly she had a lamp on the bedside table and the boxes shoved out of the way. She spread clean sheets on the bed and a colorful Mexican blanket. The bed looked inviting, and she was very tired. To rest for just a few minutes sounded like heaven.

Unable to resist the comfortable temptation, Lacy lay across the bed on top of the blanket. Almost immediately, she fell asleep.

The next thing she knew, a male voice was rumbling, "Lacy. . . Lacy. . ." in her ear.

She woke with a start to find Holt reclining on one elbow near her. "I've always had this fantasy about female politicians," he said in a low, teasing tone. "But to find a redheaded mayor in my bed is the ultimate."

"Oh! I—" She sat up, her heart fluttering, her cheeks suddenly stinging with embarrassment.

"I know. You fell asleep waiting for me."

"No! Heavens, no!" She hopped up off the bed and pushed her hair back, groping for a logical explanation. Words failed her. She stared at him. "I didn't mean to do this."

"It's okay. I'll keep quiet in the next campaign for a reasonable financial payoff. A few thou ought to do it."

"This is awful! I'm really sorry."

"Don't be. I'm not complaining. And don't worry about the payments. I'll take the money in installments." He chuckled and lay back flat on the bed, his arms flung over his head.

Even in her drowsy state, Lacy was aware of the powerful sight of his masculine form sprawled across the bed, next to the spot where she had just been. Nervously, she started laughing. "I guess I was more tired than I thought."

"I'm beat, too, but at least I'm here in Silverton, lock, stock, barrel and Jeep. I can sleep in tomorrow with no more obligations than to get settled. How's Alita?"

"She woke once. I explained that you'd be here in the morning. She went right back to sleep."

"I can't thank you enough for staying. This is definitely above and beyond the call of a mayor's duty."

"I would say 'all in a day's work,' but it has been more than usual."

"I appreciate it." He sat up, his hands resting loosely between his knees.

"Well, I'll be going now." Lacy headed for the front door. "Oh, incidentally, your neighbor in the pink house across the street would be an excellent sitter for Alita, if you can persuade her to do it. Mrs. Carson's been a widow for several years and is excellent with kids. She needs something to do and helping with Alita may be just the ticket."

"Thanks. I'll check with her tomorrow." He followed Lacy through the hallway. "That would be great if I could get someone so close to home."

Lacy liked the way he said "home," as if he'd already adopted the place. Just as she reached the door, Holt touched her hand. "Thanks again for helping today. And for taking care of Alita. And for . . . everything."

Lacy gazed up at him. In the shadowed hallway, she could see Holt's angular face and his dark, tired eyes. Her scrutiny dropped briefly to his mouth.

To Holt, in his weary state, the look was inviting. The woman was alluring. He wanted to taste. So why wait any longer? He leaned forward, letting his lips brush her cheek with a soft kiss. She felt so velvety smooth and refreshingly cool. He thought of her lips. . . .

Lacy trembled at his light caress. A part of her wanted to accept the full force of his kiss. Another part wanted to turn and run. She felt slightly dizzy with his overpowering nearness. Wildly attracted to his earthy fragrance, she wanted to fling herself into the strength he exuded. But she didn't . . . couldn't. She stood very still, waiting. . . .

Suddenly he straightened. "Oh my God."

"What's wrong?"

"I . . . I've kissed the mayor. I can't believe I was so bold."

"It was . . . nice."

" 'Nice'? Is that the best I can do?"

"Well, smooth."

"Not spectacular? No bells? Rainbows?"

"I don't have any regrets."

"That's something, I guess. I'll take what I can get. So long as the mayor doesn't think I've breached protocol."

She smiled, feeling a faint glow. "Of course not, Holt. The mayor is human, too."

"And a very alluring woman."

She turned and stepped through the door. "Good night, Holt."

"See you soon, Lacy." He watched her get in her car, turn it around in the middle of the empty street and head down the block. Undeniably, a part of him wanted to do more, much more, than kiss the mayor's cheek.

LACY POKED HER TROWEL into the soft earth. She wiggled it, pulled it out and dug in again, carefully carving out sections of rosemary. She'd kept her hands busy today, trying to occupy her mind in the process. The game she was playing with herself was to obliterate thoughts of Silverton's newest resident. But Holt Henderson's bold image wouldn't leave.

Realistically she knew that his gentle kiss had been a simple act of gratitude, coming from a man who was very tired. He probably wasn't fully aware of what he'd done and didn't even recall it today. Certainly not the way she did.

She glanced up at Sage, her white cat, who served as a silent sentinel from the back gatepost. Sage's switching tail warned Lacy that she had company. "Come on back," she called loudly to the invisible guest, who hadn't even had a chance to say a thing. "I'm out here, thinning the rosemary."

The gate creaked, but Lacy didn't bother to look up right away. Visitors this time of day were common as folks stopped to chat or bring her home-baked gifts. It was one of the little pleasures of small-town living.

"My rosemary is taking over the garden. Would you like some?" she asked.

Holt surveyed the woman down on all fours in the middle of a flower bed, her cute derriere prominent in worn-thin jeans. "Sure. I'm not much of a gardener, but I can stick it in the ground and hope for the best."

"Oh! Holt!" Lacy scrambled to her feet and wiped her hands on the seat of her jeans. "I didn't expect you. I thought it was one of my neighbors."

"Well, I am." He chuckled. "Or doesn't the end of the street qualify?"

"Of course. I just didn't think you'd . . . er, I thought you'd be too busy getting settled today to bother with your neighborhood."

"There's more to getting settled than unpacking boxes. Like finding a good sitter for Alita."

"How's she feeling today?"

"She's doing fine. There is some pain in her collar-bone area, so she isn't moving as fast as usual. But the biggest obstacle is adjusting to that clumsy harness they put on her. It's uncomfortable, but she feels better with it on than off. Mostly it helps to remind her to be care-ful."

He moved farther into the backyard, and Lacy could see that he was alone. "Where is Alita?"

"That's what I came to tell you. She's visiting Mrs. Carson now. I wanted to make sure they hit it off, just the two of them. But I liked the lady a lot."

"Mrs. Carson's very nice and extremely capable. She's been on her own for years now, and I'm sure she's lonely. That's one reason I figured she would be a good choice."

"When I left them, they were hovering over a new batch of kittens on the back porch. Alita was in heaven."

Lacy grinned and rubbed her nose with the back of her hand. "That's where I got Sage, the cat who warned me someone was coming. Mrs. Carson is Sandy Amado's mother. You met Sandy yesterday."

"Oh yes. Well, it is a small town, isn't it? Everyone seems to be related or—"

"Or they know everything about each other."

Holt's gaze traveled to the tip of Lacy's freckled nose, where she'd left a dirt smudge. "'Everything,' huh? That must be hard on a mayor's private life."

"It could be, I suppose. If the mayor had anything to hide." Lacy stuffed the plug of rosemary into a plastic bag.

"But, if the mayor was unmarried, she…or he, might want to keep some things private."

She bent and dug out a healthy section of another plant. "Here's some parsley for you. It grows well here, too."

Holt sat on a brick step and absently pulled on a nearby plant. "Speaking of keeping things private, Lacy, about last night—"

"Please don't pull that up! It's an herb."

He examined the feathery plant in his hand. "Sorry, I thought it was a weed."

"It's dill." She gestured. "Smell it."

He sniffed it and grinned in recognition. "Dill pickles. Very distinctly dill."

"As I said."

"You make your own dill pickles?"

She shook her head. "There are many other uses for dill besides pickles. It's great with lamb or fish. Gives chicken and vegetables a spark. I have a dill bread recipe that's absolutely wonderful."

"You take this stuff seriously, don't you?" He remembered the herbal iced tea she'd served in her office the day he was interviewed and looked closer at the various plants around him. "An herb garden?"

She shrugged. "It started as a supplement to my limited culinary skills. With a few sprinkles of dried dill or rosemary, plain baked chicken becomes gourmet. As I learned more about herbs and started growing them, I developed a real taste for the stronger flavors of fresh herbs. It wasn't until later that I got into edible flowers. It's really fun to watch guests' expressions when I serve a nasturtium salad or pansies and spiced, cold green beans."

He looked shocked. "Hold it. You eat flowers, too?"

"A few. Would you like to try a pansy?" She stood and dusted her hands together. "Nasturtiums are a good place to start."

"No. No, thank you. I'll stick to regular food." He looked at her quizzically. "No wonder you brought us such weird pizza yesterday. We're lucky you didn't add a few of your nasturtiums."

She grinned. "The kids might have taken to it more readily than black olives."

"I doubt it." He spread his knees and propped his elbows on them. "You are, indeed, one fascinating lady.

One I'd like to get to know better. Which brings me back to last night."

"Look, Holt, we were both tired. I shouldn't have fallen asleep on your bed. And perhaps you shouldn't have kissed me. Frankly, I would appreciate it if you'd keep those two incidents to yourself. It wouldn't look very good for the mayor, would it?"

"I'll be glad to keep them quiet. They were private incidents, and I'm a very private guy. But I'm not apologizing for kissing Her Honor. I only regret there wasn't time or energy for more."

"Why, Holt, you hardly know me."

"That's why I wanted to see if we could go to dinner sometime. Get to know each other better."

Her response was immediate. "No, I think not." It seemed that the attraction she'd felt for him had been mutual. But she couldn't let it develop. She had to halt it before it went any further.

He raised his eyebrows. "That was certainly a quick no. Is this a general policy from the mayor's office?"

"It's one of my firm rules." She fiddled with the plastic bag of herbs she'd fixed for him. "Never date employees."

"No wonder. Most of them are female. Or over seventy-five."

"It isn't professional."

"Neither is helping an employee move in. Or taking him and his daughter to the emergency room. Or staying with his daughter while he returns the moving truck." Holt pushed himself to his feet and moved closer to her. "But it's especially unprofessional for the mayor to make a male employee's bed and fall asleep on it." He stuffed his hands in his pockets, as if he had to contain them. "I'd call those actions perfectly innocent for anyone besides the mayor. Unless, as you said, the mayor is really human."

"I . . . I guess you're right." She gave him a reluctant smile. "But don't take what happened yesterday as anything except the norm. Actually, I would have done the same for anyone moving into town." She wasn't sure about that, but it sounded good.

"Oh? And the invitation in your eyes? Does that go out to just anyone?"

She opened her mouth to protest, but he took a couple of steps and was suddenly close, so close she could breathe his earthy, male fragrance. His was an aroma that appealed to her and made her senses accelerate dangerously. It made her think erotic thoughts of men and women, of her and Holt, and want to do sensuous things with him. She had the panicky feeling of losing control.

One large hand slid over hers. "You can deny it all you want to, Mayor, but it's here. Something between us. I feel it. And so do you." His words dwindled away as his lips closed over hers, and he kissed her fully and firmly on the mouth.

She swayed dizzily, not believing this was happening in her own backyard, yet unable to break away. His lips conveyed a message and hers received it, loud and clear. She feared she was transmitting the same message. He claimed he saw it in her eyes. Maybe he had. But she couldn't help it.

When he finally broke the heated contact, she felt heady with the potent power of his kiss. She didn't remember when her imagination had raged so wildly over a man. "Holt—"

He touched her bottom lip with his finger. "Now, deny *that*, Your Honor."

"No, Holt. We can't—"

"I'm afraid we already have, Lacy. About last night, you were right. The mayor *is* human." He paused. "She's warm, sensitive, receptive and can kiss like a dream." He took the plastic bag of herbs from her limp hand and strode to the gate. Before walking through it, he turned around. "You haven't heard the last of this. I don't give up easily on something that interests me— and you interest me, Mayor."

"That's becoming pretty obvious."

"I'm determined that we'll get to know each other better. Even if we have to do it in your herb garden, which seems to be your comfort zone." He paused with a saucy grin. "Frolicking in the flowers sounds imaginative. I might even be enticed to try a nasturtium if you'd allow yourself to be enticed by a new employee."

Before she could voice her indignation, he was gone.

5

ALTHOUGH LACY would have preferred a little distance from this man who dominated her thoughts and stimulated her imagination, she and Holt were together almost constantly. Getting him established was part of her job, and first thing Monday morning, she showed him his office. It was across the hall from hers.

"Hope you don't mind sharing with our Economic Development Department." Lacy flipped on a couple of lights. "This is the only room on this floor besides the ones I use that's equipped with phone service and typewriters and electricity."

Holt surveyed the long, narrow office, which was large enough for several desks. There were only two, so the place looked pretty empty. "This is Economic Development?"

"It's a small department consisting of one. She's creating her job as she goes along. We figured there was no sense in keeping the whole building going if we weren't using it, so we cut the electricity in the unused portions of the courthouse." She glanced at him hopefully. "Holt, we're a struggling town. That means we don't have the funds for excess expenses. The head of Economic Development is donating her time. That's the kind of dedication we have around here."

"Sure. I understand. And I don't mind sharing at all. This office is fine. I won't be in it much, anyway. There's plenty of room for both of us." He rubbed his hands together as he walked to the windows that lined the opposite wall. "Nice view."

"You can observe the historic district from this office and oversee the progress of your work." She felt relieved that he was so understanding.

"Well, I won't be doing much overseeing. As the only member of my department, I'll be out there working." His gaze swept the room again. "I would like a drawing table, in addition to a desk, though. And a better lighting system."

"See Annie about those things." Lacy backed to the door. "I have to attend a meeting right now. If you need anything, just ask Annie."

"Is Annie the secretary?"

"She's the Economic Development Department." Lacy looked back over her shoulder with a grin. "Annie's a wheeler-dealer extraordinaire. She got an air conditioner donated to my office when mine broke and we had no funds to cover a new one. Oh, incidentally, we don't have secretaries. Hope you can type."

"Don't need to," Holt mumbled, already speculating on his ever-changing situation. Before he had a chance to check out his desk, clunking sounds and the rustle of papers accompanied a feminine groan. A woman with wild strawberry-blond hair struggled through the door, her arms loaded with bags and boxes.

"Here, let me help you." Automatically he reached out, and she dumped the whole mess in his arms.

"Thanks. Just put them over here." She led the way to one of the desks and scooted everything else aside. "This job gets more and more curious. Never thought I'd be inspecting pot holders and hand-painted tea towels and Granny's knitting, but here I am." She gave him a wide smile and extended her hand. "I'm Annie Clayton."

He shook her hand, stunned by this whirlwind who smelled like apples. "Nice to meet you, Annie. I'm Holt Henderson."

"Hope you don't mind sharing. I'm only here three half days a week."

"Not at all. I won't be here much, anyway."

"So it's not necessary that we're entirely compatible? That's good. Because I'm not much of a desk person. I tend to spread out all over the place."

"That makes two of us."

"Well, nuts! If neither of us likes offices, what are we doing here?" Her green eyes danced with laughter.

"We need a place to put our stuff, I guess." He liked her forthright nature.

Annie laughed aloud. "Brother harry! Do I have the stuff!" She picked up a cute handmade clown. "Now would you buy this for your little girl? We have a campaign in town to start people thinking about how they can contribute to Silverton's economy. Get Busy with a Business. Do you think it's a good slogan?"

"Sounds good to me. Looks like it's working."

"Well, this group of enterprising ladies wants to have a craft shop. They've even picked a name. Granny's Attic. Cute, huh?" She lifted a clown and wrinkled her nose. "What do you think?"

He gave her an exaggerated shrug. "What do I know about dillydallies? Fixing up old buildings is my field."

She scrutinized the next item, a pot holder mitten in the vague shape of a Holstein cow, complete with pink udders and black-and-white spots. "Thanks for the input."

"Anytime."

"This is pretty clever. You wouldn't want a puppy, would you?"

"What?" He was caught off guard.

"It's a dalmatian. These spots reminded me. Cutest pup you've ever, ever seen."

He rubbed his face with his palm. "I wish you hadn't said that."

"Why?"

"Because all my daughter has talked about since she knew we were moving to a real house with a yard was having a puppy."

"Oh really?" Annie dropped the pot holder and launched into one of her favorite subjects. "This little pup was the runt of the litter, and I was never able to sell her. Plus, she has a flaw. Her ear is bent, just a little. It isn't bad, but keeps her from being show quality. Actually, it gives her a darling expression. I can't keep her. But I want to find a good home for her."

"Give me time to think about it."

"She's free to a good home. And I'm sure you'd provide one."

Holt walked to the window, then back to Annie's cluttered desk. "A female? That means more puppies in a year or so unless—"

"I'll take care of that for you. I have an excellent vet, and he gives me a deal because I always use him for my dogs. A female dog will be a nice pet for a child. She won't be too aggressive. This one already has a nice disposition."

"Sounds like a reasonable deal, but I'm not saying yes. If you find a good home for her, by all means, let her go."

"Right. No rush." Annie paused. "Maybe you'd like to bring your daughter out to the farm this weekend.

We have pumpkins growing that'll be ready for Halloween in a couple of months. She could pick one out, and we'd put her name on it. Then, near the end of October, she could come out and pick up her very own pumpkin, for carving into a jack-o'-lantern. While she's there, she could take a look at the puppy and see if she likes it."

"I see through that method." Holt eyed her skeptically. "Wise tactic. One look at that pup, and Alita wouldn't be able to resist. And I'd be a heel if I refused."

Annie shrugged and grinned broadly. "It was worth a try. The invitation for the pumpkin still holds. And I'll hide the pup from your daughter if you bring her out."

"No promises." He raised both hands and walked back to his desk. "I'll let you know."

"Now I see why Lacy wanted to hire you. You definitely make a great winning strategy." She laid her finger along her cheek and studied him purposely.

"What are you talking about?" Holt drew back.

"No offense, now, Holt.... We're hurting here in Silverton. And we're desperate for help and heroes and ... everything! So, we—actually Lacy—devised a 'winning strategy.' And you're it." She smiled at him proudly.

"I didn't realize."

"Well, you're not *all*, but you're a big part of it. The rest of us are just pawns in the great Silverton chess game. But you—*you're* the king. If you don't get that historic district in shape, we're down the tubes. But, after all that Lacy claimed about your abilities, I'm sure you can do it. She has a great deal of confidence in you, Holt." Annie continued sorting through her bundles.

"Now, I have to decide if these handmade things are of high enough quality to sell in a craft shop. Such a strange business. What do I know about this stuff? Apples are my game."

Holt watched her for a few minutes, feeling a variety of emotions that ranged from pride to anger. "I was supposed to see you about getting a drafting table and better lighting in here. A couple of crookneck lamps should do it."

Annie made a note. "I'll see what I can find."

"Thanks." Holt stared out the window at the dilapidated historic district behind the courthouse. *Thank you, Annie, for being so brutally honest.* The anger began to dominate his emotions. Lacy Donahue was something else. She had elaborated on a friendly relationship to make him feel especially welcome, as if he were a part of the town from day one. Suddenly, he felt very manipulated by her. *What else am I going to discover about this job and you, Mayor Donahue?*

He decided to confront her with what he'd learned and was waiting in her office when Lacy returned from her meeting. "I'd like to have a word with you."

"Sure." She motioned for him to have a seat and proceeded to fix them both a glass of iced tea. "What's up? Did you meet Annie? You two haven't had a spat already, have you?"

"Oh no. Everything's fine with Annie. And I honestly don't mind sharing that office with her. We figure neither of us will be there enough to matter."

Lacy handed him a large Styrofoam cup filled with iced tea. "That's what I thought, too. So what's the problem, Holt? You look disturbed."

He gulped half the tea, then set the cup on the table and gazed at her solemnly for a few moments. "The 'winning strategy,' Lacy?"

"Oh damn! That Annie has a big mouth!" Lacy slapped her thigh and sighed heavily.

"No. She's just honest. Which is more than you can say for some people in high office."

"Oh, Holt, please don't be offended. We're just so desperate for someone strong. We discussed you—"

"Great! You sat around discussing me?"

"You bet. We wanted someone who could be a leader." Her expression grew serious. "We *need* a good leader. You won."

"Don't try flattery at this point, Lacy. What other assets were you looking for? Male, muscular and strong? Younger than seventy-five?"

"Holt! That's not fair!"

"All of this fake friendship stuff isn't fair, either. I fell for it. When all along you were just patting my fanny so I'd do a job for you." He stood and glared down at her. "There's another term for such action, but I won't say it."

"Holt, there wasn't any 'fake friendship.' Honest. Whatever happened or was said between us was real. And private. When I said we discussed you, I meant that we discussed your assets—your career assets. And what you could offer Silverton."

"I like to know when I'm being used, that's all." He turned toward the door.

She rushed forward and caught his wrist and held it firmly. The muscle in his forearm tightened. "Holt, I'll admit it. You *are* being used. We need you and a thousand like you so badly. There're only a few old diehards like us in Silverton. And now we have you. But the bottom line is that we desperately needed you, and you came along." She lifted her shoulders in a shrug. "We just took advantage of a good thing. Now if you can't live with that, with how we hired you, with what we want you to do for us, maybe you'd better head out now."

His lips tightened. She could be tough. But what did he expect from the mayor of a dying town? A real tough cookie. "I'm staying. I just had to get that off my chest."

She sighed and squeezed his wrist, letting her hand slide down to his. "Thank you. I think we got a real winner in Holt Henderson."

"I want to be appreciated for me, not for what you and your staff in some glorified moment created for me. I'm just a man here to do a job. That's all. And if it works for Silverton, that's great. If not, so be it. I will have done my job to the best of my ability."

"That's all we can ask." She still held his hand. It felt warm and strong, and she didn't want to let go. But a part of her knew she couldn't go around holding her employees' hands. "I'm sorry if you were offended."

"I think the terms Annie used grated on me. And maybe the responsibility, too. But you've smoothed it over. You're a good politician, Lacy."

She released his hand and dropped hers by her side. "You make it sound like a dirty job."

"Not the way you do it. But it's obvious the town mayor has a certain loyalty."

"When I was elected to this position, I took that mandate seriously. I pledged my loyalty to this town and especially to these people. And I'm fighting tooth and nail to save it. Maybe someday, Holt, when you've lived here awhile, you'll feel some of that loyalty."

"Maybe. Meantime, I have a job to do."

"You're going to do fine, Holt. I just know it."

"Oh? Well, when can we discuss a plan for the remodeling? I want to make a priority list of buildings and decide on a central theme for color and design. Is there a committee that will meet with me and keep track of progress?"

"How about us? You and me. Are we enough of a committee? I don't have many folks who are available on a regular basis during the week. We even have town council meetings on Saturday to include those members who work out of town."

"Sure." He shrugged. "You seem to know what you want done with the district."

"I do." She smiled confidently. "How about Wednesday? That'll give you a little time to get settled."

"That'll give me time to do a few sketches." He paused before leaving. "Thank you, Your Honor. I'm glad we had this little chat."

Lacy smiled weakly. She felt that they were treading on thin ice with him. Just when things started looking good, something happened to make him readjust his thinking about Silverton. But this time, his jabs had been directed at her personally and the budding friendship they had been developing since he arrived. She couldn't really blame him. The truth looked bad.

They *had* set out to find a winning strategy. And when they came up with Holt, Lacy wasn't about to let him go. Only now, the secret was out, and his trust in her was tainted. She had known that putting him in the office with Annie would be risky. Annie was so damned honest, she was short of being diplomatic.

Lacy sighed heavily and felt as if she'd lied to a best friend. Now why would she feel that way? She hardly knew Holt Henderson. He wasn't her best friend. He was her employee, and she'd better remember it.

ON WEDNESDAY MORNING, Holt appeared in her office with several rough sketches filled with prospects and directions for the remodeling he had in mind. Lacy listened and observed as he spread the designs on her desk and explained each one. He had good ideas, and he expressed them stoutly, even when they conflicted with hers.

"I think we should start with the bank building." He pulled out the rough draft of the circle of buildings that would be renovated in the first phase. "It's centrally located and has the most interesting history."

"That has nothing to do with it," Lacy insisted. "All of those buildings have interesting histories when you delve into them. The Sonoran adobe on the end used to be a hospital. Then it was a boarding school. In the twenties and thirties, it was a pool hall."

"Did Pancho Villa shoot a few games of pool before he took hostages in the bank?" Holt challenged.

"No, but some of our residents may have relatives who went to the school or were born in the hospital. Some even shot pool. It'll be familiar to them."

"If I remember our original conversation correctly, we're trying to draw outsiders, not just hold on to the old diehards, as you call yourselves, of Silverton." He pushed the sketch before her. "Look, the old bank has good lines. Shows the Spanish influence in this area. Those beautiful arches in the front with the long porch and the decorative tile . . . they'll finish out beautifully. It'll be a good showcase for our work. Better than the plain adobe."

"I know, Holt," she said softly. "You're absolutely right. It will be beautiful when refinished. But we want it done right. And I'm afraid we don't have enough money at the present. The adobe has a much simpler style and is a good, solid building. It will probably need less work than the rest."

"It's an ordinary rectangle. Almost no style."

"Yes, but I already have an interested party who—"

"There! That's influencing your reasoning." He sat back with a disgusted sigh. "It's a political decision, not an artistic one."

She tightened her lips. "In case you've forgotten, I am in a political office. And I have to oversee the whole town, not just what one person wants. Yes, it's political. But that's how things get done around here."

"Okay, it's the Sonoran adobe first." He sighed in resignation. "What's the interest? Could you at least tell me that?"

She hesitated, then decided it would only be fair to tell him a little of the situation from her side. "There are a couple of businessmen from out of town who are very interested in starting a restaurant. They want to create an upscale, authentic Mexican restaurant with lots of style and atmosphere and excellent cuisine. They'd be willing to lease the Sonoran adobe if the completed building is suitable. The catch is that we have to prove that we are going to be able to draw outsiders."

"And how do you propose to do that?"

"We hope to have complete citizen participation as visible proof of our good intentions. And as soon as the adobe is finished and the investors see that it will house a nice restaurant, we hope to start on the old hotel, so people coming here can have a place to stay."

He nodded silently. "Okay. Your town. Your plan. Enough said."

She leaned forward on the table and ticked off items on her fingers. "I'm trying to get more money for this project through grants and other means. But Holt, we have to go slow and easy at first. One building. Try to find an occupant. Get it producing. Establish the funds for another building. Find another occupant . . . et cetera. As soon as the money comes through, I'll give you the green light to start another building. But until then, we're forced to go with what we can handle now, which is the simpler adobe."

"I understand. No objections, Your Honor. The first thing I'll need is a small crew for demolition and cleanup. Where can I hire—"

She shook her head. "I . . . at present, I don't have sufficient funds for that. But the local Kiwanis club has volunteered to serve as a work crew this Saturday. You would need to supervise."

He winced. "Ah, I see. Okay. Not a great start, is it? No budget. No crew. No subs. Otherwise, I get to call the shots and be my own boss." He lifted his hands and let them fall on his thighs in an act of frustration.

"With a little help, it shouldn't take too long, should it?"

He shrugged. "I'm not immune to labor."

"Holt . . ." She paused and gave him a little smile. "Thanks for being so understanding."

"Sure." He rose from the table and started for the office door. "Uh, I figure loser buys dinner. And I'm not the winner of this session. Would you consent to—"

She stood, an apologetic expression on her face. "Holt, please don't."

"Oh, the old mayor-doesn't-date routine again, huh?" His gray eyes latched on to hers. "Another time, for sure. I don't give up easily, Lacy. And I don't give a damn about your personal rules."

She didn't agree. Nor did she disagree. She watched him leave the room with her emotions tumbling. Would she agree another time? Or would he give up on her before she relented? She couldn't answer. This was one subject on which the mayor couldn't make a decision.

FRIDAY AFTERNOON a torrential rain hit Silverton. It didn't take the phone call from the Cultural Arts League for Lacy to know the evening's performance would have to be canceled. It was just as well. She had tons of new material to read and decide on. If she'd gone to the play, her mind would have been on work that needed doing. Wrapped in a brown raincoat, her briefcase filled to the brim with paperwork, she darted to her car after work.

Once home, she changed into her favorite worn jeans, an overlarge blue shirt and warm, sloppy socks. Feeling comfortable and relaxed, she aimed for the kitchen, where she fixed herself a cup of hot, orange-mint tea. Then she settled into the big cushioned chair by the corner lamp with a six-inch pile of reports on grants available to cities like Silverton, which she'd just received from the federal government. Sage curled on the sofa and dozed.

As Lacy was losing herself in *Grant Options for Small Municipalities*, someone rang her doorbell. Lacy murmured to Sage, who switched her tail and waited cautiously for the visitors.

The rain was so heavy and the sky so dark that Lacy couldn't distinguish the shadowy figures on her porch through the window. She opened the door to the very wet, tall figure of Holt Henderson. He wore a drenched cowboy hat and a black leather jacket that was shiny and slick. Beads of rain peppered his face like freckles. Beside him, sitting in a large red wagon with her legs curled between several plastic grocery bags, was Alita, draped in a blanket.

"Hi!" The little girl's large gray eyes flashed from beneath the blanket. "We've come for our rain check!"

"What?" Lacy's gaze flew from Alita to Holt.

"I explained to Alita," he began, "that a rain check just meant a delay of delivery. Usually it happens later, but in this case, the rain made it happen now. I figured that if the Cultural Arts League drama canceled tonight, which it did, you'd be willing to do a hamburger fry with us."

"Holt—" She started to laugh.

"Now, I know we can't do a backyard barbecue, but we're much more flexible than the Cultural Arts League. No costumes or anything. My part of the rain check is that I'll cook the burgers on the back porch on my portable charcoal grill, which I happened to bring along. I'm afraid we'll have to make the picnic in your kitchen." He paused to assess her reception. "If you don't mind."

"We brought all the stuff," Alita added. "And we'll clean up afterward."

"Well, of course." Lacy pushed open the screen door without hesitation. How could she refuse such an appealing, unique offer? "Come on in and get dry." As she helped Alita out of her blanket and coat, she said, "Have you met my cat, Sage? She's been looking forward to meeting you, Alita."

When the little girl walked into the living room to search for the cat, Lacy caught Holt's gaze. "Clever. To use a child," she mumbled.

"I figured it was a strategy that would work." He followed her into the house with an armload of supplies from the wagon. "And it did."

"You admit it! You admit using her."

"Everybody else around here uses strategies. Why shouldn't I? Sometimes it's necessary. You said so yourself." He smiled pleasantly and handed her one of the bags that was slipping. "I hope we didn't interrupt anything important tonight."

"I was studying how to get more money for the renovation project. *Grant Options for Small Municipalities* makes fascinating reading on a rainy night."

He rolled his eyes. "Sounds dry as a bone."

"This sounds—" she grinned up at him "—much better."

"It will be. Guaranteed!"

Alita came to meet them. "Where's your kitty, Lacy? She's hiding from me!" Her little girl's voice sounded loud and shrill.

Lacy smiled and tucked her arm around Alita. "Sage isn't used to a lot of noise. But I'll bet we can coax her out. Call her softly."

In a few minutes the frightened cat responded to Lacy's soft encouragement and began a reluctant friendship with the ebullient Alita.

Lacy left the cat and child to get acquainted and motioned for Holt to accompany her into the kitchen.

"Excuse my rambunctious daughter," he murmured.

"Sage is just spoiled. Sometimes I think it's too quiet and peaceful around here." Lacy switched on the kitchen light.

"A little calming female influence wouldn't hurt my daughter." Holt piled the bags on the counter and looked around. "You have a nice place, Lacy. It's larger than mine."

"I don't know what possessed me to buy it. I rattle around in here. It's much too large for me." She shrugged. "But I like the house a lot."

"It's befitting the mayor." Holt nodded with approval. "Needs a little fix up, but—" he chuckled "—that's another job."

"Maybe when you finish the historic district, you'll take on the residential."

"Sounds like you want to keep me busy."

"I want to keep you around." Only when the words were out did Lacy realize how that sounded. She quickly changed the subject. "How was Alita's first week at school? And how did things go with Mrs. Carson?"

Holt seemed eager to talk. "That lady is fantastic with kids. Alita tried to use her clavicle injury as an excuse not to go to school the first day. She wanted me to stay home with her. I suppose it's natural for a kid. But I felt she was trying to manipulate me, and I insisted that she go to school. Then she had the teacher call me from school to say that she was having a bad day and would I please come get her?" He shook his head. "I sent Mrs. Carson, instead. She took care of everything just great. By the time I got home after work, Alita was happy as a clam at Mrs. Carson's. They were making doughnuts in the kitchen when I got there."

"I'm glad it's working out, Holt."

"You were right about Mrs. C. She's excellent. Thanks for recommending her."

Lacy rubbed her hand on her thighs nervously. Being alone with Holt again made her realize just how much she reacted to him. "Well, shall we fix hamburgers? Did you say you brought a little grill?"

Everyone worked together and before long, the savory aroma of grilling hamburgers drifted from the porch. Lacy turned on the radio and set Alita up on an assembly line of buns. "There you go, my dear. Squirt, smear and pile to your heart's content."

"What do you like on yours?"

"Everything!"

"Whee!" Alita giggled as she squeezed mustard in decorative circles on the buns. "Everything!"

Lacy joined Holt on the porch to check on the hamburgers' progress. "How's the chef doing?"

He gave her a long look. "The wind blows rain on the fire, drenches the blaze and ruins the burgers. I'm having a ball." Holt flipped one patty with the spatula. "I do hope we aren't intruding on your evening, Your Honor."

"Not at all. I'm glad you came."

"If it'll make you feel any better, this is the happiest I've seen Alita all week."

"It's been a traumatic week for her. Moving and breaking her clavicle all in one day isn't easy for a six-year-old." Lacy glanced into the kitchen, where the little girl appeared to be having fun drawing mustard and ketchup designs on the buns. "She seems fine now."

"In your blessed company—"

"Spare me!" Lacy said laughingly. "I'd better help Alita with the buns, or they'll never be ready."

By the end of the evening, Lacy felt much more at ease with Holt. She could admit that she'd had fun. Eventually Alita had made friends with Sage and seemed to enjoy being around Lacy. They all pitched in to clean the kitchen, and when it was done, Holt announced it was time to go. Lacy felt a pang of regret that the evening was soon to end. Alita begged to stay longer and made a big to-do of saying good-night to Sage.

Lacy reluctantly walked Holt to the door. "I'm glad you brought her over here, Holt. And you're a promising chef. If the historical district doesn't keep you busy enough, maybe you can hire on as the chef in the restaurant."

He frowned. "Are you trying to tell me something? Is the historic renovation plan going sour?"

"No. Not at all. I have complete confidence in you."

He looked at her closely. "You have this all planned, don't you Lacy?"

"Not everything." She hadn't expected to enjoy the evening so much. And she certainly hadn't planned on her emotions rushing to embrace him.

"This?" He whispered and brushed his lips against hers. "Did you plan on this?" He kissed her more substantially this time, letting his lips play along hers with soft kisses before encompassing them completely.

Lacy stood spellbound, arms limp by her sides, her face upturned to him, enjoying the intoxicating drink of his kiss. When he finally lifted his head, she responded softly, "No, Holt. This was definitely not in the plan."

"Some things are better that way."

"You know how I feel about—"

Alita's shrill voice interrupted. "Are you two finished?"

Holt stepped back and mumbled in a low voice. "Yes, honey. Are we ready to go?"

"I've already said good-night to Sage," she said, yawning.

Holt wrapped Alita in the blanket and lifted her into the wagon. Then he turned to Lacy as he slid one arm into his black jacket. His words were intended only for her. "I'll admit to using her to get to you, Lacy. It was my 'strategy' for spending a 'winning' evening with you. Clever, huh? Next time though, I hope we can be alone."

She opened her mouth, then closed it into a tight little grin. "Your 'strategy,' Holt?"

He touched her lower lip, running his finger along it. "Don't say anything. It worked for both of us, didn't it?"

She nodded. "You're devious."

"No. I'm honest."

"Daadee. . . ." Alita whined.

"See you. I have a big day with my Kiwanis crew tomorrow."

"I may stop by to see how things are going."

"Please do, Your Honor. We'd love to have you join our cleanup crew. Hope this rain lets up." Holt effortlessly lifted the entire wagon off the porch, and, hunching his square shoulders against the drizzle, pulled the wagon down the street.

Lacy watched them disappear with distinct feelings of regret. What was wrong with her, anyway? This man was a city employee, and she had rules about this sort of activity. Plus, she had her own private set of rules, and they didn't include becoming involved with a man who had a child who needed a mo—

She stepped back inside and slammed the door. *Don't say it! Don't even think it! You can't! You've already ruined one potentially happy family! And this one's definitely better off without you.*

Lacy sank into her chair. The government reports she'd been reading were scattered. The tea she'd prepared was now cold and forgotten. Her evening had been occupied with Holt and his daughter—completely and fully.

She realized all too clearly that Holt made her feel as no other man had in years. Happy. But she couldn't make him happy in the end. So she'd better stop it now.

THE NEXT DAY dawned sunny for the cleanup crew. Holt supervised thirty enthusiastic Kiwanis members in a demolition of the old, dilapidated parts of the Sonoran adobe building. Sometime around midafternoon, Lacy made a quick stop that included a brief thumbs-up appreciation speech.

As he watched and listened to her, Holt had to admire the spitfire redhead who had captured his waking hours and now had started to haunt his nights.

Amazingly, Lacy had enticed her audience into spending their day off working hard for their town, promising it would come back to them if Silverton made it. She was a damn good politician. Good for Silverton. And good for him and Alita, whether she believed it or not.

Holt spent the afternoon thinking of her, knowing he had to do something about their stalemate. But what? One evening of hamburgers wouldn't do it. He'd have to think of something else.

6

"I CAN'T BELIEVE you all got so much done in one weekend." Lacy preceded Holt into the echoingly empty adobe building. She had requested a Monday morning walk-through so she could evaluate the quality of work done by her experimental system of volunteers.

Holt moved into step with her, his leather boots clumping on the bare concrete floors. "I'll admit I had reservations about this, but the group on Saturday was terrific. They came here to work, and indeed they did. Several even came back on Sunday with their pickup trucks, and we hauled away loads of trash."

"I didn't mean to saddle you with a bunch of novices, but I knew we couldn't afford to hire a crew for you right now. And when the Kiwanis group asked what they could do to help, I naturally said, 'Come and work.'"

"It was a good idea, Mayor." He stepped over a small pile of wood and plaster scraps. "As you can see, I still have some cleanup work. A good bit of the interior mess appeared to be caused by someone, or ones, who had used the empty building as a shelter."

"You mean vagrants?" Lacy looked shocked. "I'm not aware of any homeless people around here."

"We figured somebody had used it only occasionally, not all the time. There was even a fire pit in the corner of one of the back rooms."

"They started a fire on the floor?" She was quite alarmed by that news.

"It would be too obvious to use the fireplace and have the smoke go up the chimney. Parts of the ceiling and roof are missing in that room, so I'm sure they found it easier to conceal the smoke by letting it drift out. It wasn't a very big fire area."

"But there's the potential for a destructive fire in the building if vagrants use it that way. We simply can't have that. Show me where it is."

"Actually, it was pretty safe since the floor's concrete." Holt led the way to the back room, where all that remained was a blackened spot on the concrete floor. "As you can see, it's all been cleaned up. There were a couple of old mattresses and junk." He walked to the far corner and inspected the ceiling. "Now that I'm working here daily, I can keep a close eye on the place, and, before long, we'll be able to secure the building."

Lacy stared at the charred floor with a frustrated sigh. She peered out the nearby open window frames. "It'd be easy for someone to get in, wouldn't it? I'll speak to Sheriff Meyer about this. Maybe he can patrol it more often."

"Right. But I don't think they'll return now that we've intruded on their territory and cleaned them out. Getting that job done Saturday allows me to move forward with the schedule, Lacy. It's slower than if I had a regular crew, but we're progressing, just the same. By next week, I'll be ready to start on the exterior and roof repair."

"Just getting this much done makes the possibility seem like a reality to me." Lacy turned in a circle in the middle of the room, the light of hope visible on her face. "It isn't in awful shape, is it?"

"Not too bad. The fact that the building has been used at various points in past years has kept it in better condition than most hundred-year-old buildings." He looked around the room, then back to her with a glisten in his eyes. "Oh, yes. It's possible, Lacy. If you get this thrilled when we merely clean it out, you're going to love the finished product."

She clasped her hands and smiled at him. "I knew you could do this, Holt. I just knew it!"

He watched her, trying to remind himself that she was his boss and the mayor. This was actually a progress meeting, and she was here to assess information on his work progress. "I'll repair the roof first. It'll require draw pipes projecting from the parapets to drain rainwater from the finished roof and keep the ceiling from leaking."

"Then you'll move your work to the inside?"

Her blue eyes worked a terrible magic on his libido, and Holt felt his attention meandering. He tried to remain on the subject of the renovation. "The first interior job will be to brace or shore up the walls. Then I'll fit the doors and windows with heavy wooden frames."

"This old mud adobe crumbles over the years, doesn't it?" She ran her hand along one wall, and grit fell to the floor.

He nodded. "I'll probably use concrete plaster, even though it isn't as authentic as mud plaster, because of the economic value. Otherwise, it would have to be replastered every few years, especially with heavy rains."

"Right...." She gazed solemnly at him.

Suddenly he turned away and rocked back on his heels. "Lacy, this isn't working."

"What, Holt?" She moved to his side. "What's wrong?"

He turned to her and, without another word, only a certain desperate look in his eyes, took her in his arms. "This...." he whispered. "Staying apart." Then he kissed her, long and hard. When he lifted his head, his voice was low and intense. "Your rule about not dating employees is ridiculous. How often does the opportunity come around? We have to do something about changing it."

Her hands rested on his chest, and she felt the heart-pounding warmth of his body. How often, indeed? And how often did she feel this way about a man? "Wh-what do you suggest?"

"Go away with me. This weekend. We'll go to Cloudcroft. Don't tell anyone where you're going. No one will guess we're together. It'll be a hideaway. I know the perfect place."

"Holt, we hardly know each other. We haven't even had a real date. And you want me to spend the weekend with you?"

"Why not? We know each other better than most. We're together all the time. I see you every day. And I'm going crazy keeping my distance and acting like we're casual acquaintances."

"In a way, we are."

"No, we aren't. Anyway, it isn't enough for me. Oh, Lacy...." He sighed and aligned her thighs with his. "Come with me. Give us a chance to know each other without the constant intrusions of our lives. Alita is always with me. And your job is impossible. It monopolizes all of your time and attention. As long as we stay here, there'll be no privacy."

"Holt, you're fantasizing. I'm a very practical person."

"So am I. That's why I think we need to get away from all this reality so we can give our relationship a chance to blossom."

"But, Holt—"

"No 'buts.' Forget you're the mayor for the weekend. I'll forget I'm a very responsible father."

"What'll you do about Alita?"

"I'll get Mrs. Carson to stay with her. I'll leave my daughter if you'll leave your job and your ever-loving responsibilities to everybody in this town. It'll be a minivacation that we both need. And maybe . . . just maybe something nice will result."

"You're very convincing, Holt." Her head was spinning, and she couldn't believe that she was actually considering his bold scheme. Maybe that's why it appealed to her. It was an unconventional thing for her to do. She'd never left town without letting anyone know where she was and how long she'd be gone. And furthermore, everyone in town always knew who was accompanying her or who she was visiting. But this little adventure with Holt sounded daring and exciting.

"Say yes, Lacy." His lips teased hers.

"Oh, Holt, I don't know."

"It'll be okay. Just the two of us."

"Well . . ." She could feel herself weakening. "I can't believe I'm thinking this."

"Is that a yes?"

"Yes. . . ." Her voice was barely audible.

"Lacy . . ." His lips closed tightly over hers, and his all-encompassing kiss left no doubt about his desires.

As she responded to the warmth he exuded, Lacy felt those same desires for the first time in years. And it felt fabulous.

THE FOLLOWING SATURDAY dawned crisp and blue-skied, with the feel of New Mexico autumn in the air. Lacy didn't remember the colors ever being so brilliant. The mountains were painted with a dozen shades of gold, interspersed with deep green from the pines and crimson from the oaks.

Lacy considered pinching herself to see if the much-anticipated time was here, if she was actually in Holt Henderson's Jeep, zipping out of town with him. It was unlike her, this spontaneous decision to leave her responsibilities and personal obligations behind. But she had done it. Only Mrs. Carson knew that they were together and where they were going.

Lacy glanced at Holt beside her. He looked so self-assured, as if he definitely belonged here, guiding the Jeep, taking her away. Maybe it was the right decision. She felt too good for it to be wrong.

Her gaze traveled over his sexy, masculine body: his broad shoulders, his muscular arms and sturdy hands, his legs, which stretched out forever. . . .

Only now, as they whizzed through the golden autumn landscape to an unknown experience in the mountains, would she let herself appreciate and enjoy his maleness. She realized that after her divorce she had closed men out of her life. It was easy to do in Silverton, since opportunities were slim. But she also knew that it had been too long. Far too long.

She leaned back and heaved a shaky little sigh in an attempt to relax.

He gave her a brief glance with an encouraging smile.

She tried to return the smile, but her apprehension got in the way. Her gaze settled on his hands: capable, wide-fingered, hard-working hands. She reached out and softly touched the one nearest her.

"It feels good, doesn't it, Lacy, to leave it all behind?"

"Yes." She let her hand drop to the compartment between them. "It's beautiful up here, especially this time of year."

"Do you come often?"

"I used to make this trip a couple of times a year with a friend from Silverton who owned a cabin in Cloudcroft."

Holt was quiet for a long moment. Then, as if he couldn't help himself, he blurted, "A man? Was this friend a man?" Then he lifted his hand from the steering wheel and motioned for her to be quiet. "No, Lacy. That was stupid and jealous of me. Please don't answer that. I don't know what got into me."

Lacy tried to make light of Holt's jealousy. "It's all right. My friend was a woman. In fact, there were several of us who would go to the cabin. Some, like Sandy, were married. A couple were divorced, like me. It was great fun and usually we had an adventure or two before we got back to civilization."

Holt chuckled, strangely relieved. What was wrong with him? Of course she'd had relationships since her divorce. It was only natural. So what difference did it make now? She was with him. "What kind of adventure? A flat tire?"

She smiled wryly. "Stuck in the mud. But we managed by a rather unconventional way to get unstuck."

"Okay, I'll bite. How?"

"One particularly wet autumn, it rained all weekend. We were content to sit by the fire and talk and relax, but when we were ready to leave Sunday afternoon, we realized that all four of our cars were stuck in the most god-awful, gunky mud you've ever seen."

"Gumbo?"

"Yes, that's what they call it. We were up to our hubcaps, and it looked like we'd be there all week! Well, we had to leave to return to work. So, we found a way out."

"I can't imagine how, unless . . ."

"You're probably on the right track. One of the neighbors who lives there year-round had a very large snowplow in his yard. Apparently he drove it for the county in the winter."

"Don't tell me you got him to push you out!"

"Yep. And it worked fine."

Holt laughed and shook his head. "What a sight that must have been."

"Another time, one of the ladies broke her leg skiing. Four of us had gone together in my little Toyota. Getting her home with a full leg cast in my compact car was quite a trick!"

"Oh, so you ski?"

"Not very well, but I'm game. Do you?" She imagined from his obvious body strength that he would.

But he shook his head. "Not downhill. Occasionally I cross-country. Ruined my knees in high school football. The stress of downhill is too risky. Guess that's a sign of maturity, when risks outweigh the fun."

"I guess." Her eyes inadvertently went to his knees. Of course, she couldn't see anything particular about his legs, except that his jeans looked new. A sharp crease ran up the middle of each leg, growing faint where the material stretched tightly across his thighs. "Have you been up here before, Holt?"

"My brothers and I lived up here half the time when we were growing up in El Paso. But I haven't been back in several years."

She noted the way his walnut-colored hair hugged his neck in back, an inch or so slipping inside his collar. "Is this a nostalgia trip for you, Holt? Did you and your wife come up here?"

"No. I wouldn't do that to you, Lacy." His eyes gazed straight ahead, his expression impassive. "I want this to be a chance for us to create our own special memories. Cloudcroft is ours, Lacy. I hope we'll look back on this weekend as a wonderful beginning."

"I hope so, too," she murmured in a soft-voiced admission.

He looked great today in a khaki sweater, its buttoned neckline open. She stared at that spot, where a few curly edges of dark chest hair sought freedom. Suddenly she wanted to see more of him, to touch that chest and run her fingers along his lean body. She also wanted to feel his broad hands on her, to taste his gentle kiss.

As if he could read her mind, he placed his hand on hers. She turned her hand palm up to match his, and their fingers laced, his large tanned hand engulfing her slender pale one. It was a small act, but it seemed beautifully significant. Reassuring. Secure. Sensuous.

"So, what position did you play in football?"

He quirked one eyebrow. "Would you know if I told you?"

"I might. I just wondered how you hurt your knees. Did you have surgery?"

"Yep. Both knees." He looked at her with a grin. "Is this the part where we find out about each other's past?"

She felt embarrassed as well as a little angry. Her response was testy and defensive. "Well, I don't know much about you, Holt, except that your wife died five years ago and you have a six-year-old daughter."

"I don't know much about you, either, Lacy, except that you're divorced from someone in Fort Worth."

"Aren't you curious?"

He took a breath. "About you? Yes. But not about him. I don't want to know any more about him than I know now. I guess it's because I want you all to myself. I want our relationship to begin the day we met—no baggage, no past memories, good, bad or indifferent. And no regrets."

"Okay." Although Lacy was curious about Holt, his statement gave her tremendous relief. It meant she wouldn't have to reveal any more about herself than he already knew. None of her past secrets would have to come out to spoil what they had together. It could be just the two of them, plain and simple, from this day forth. Maybe this kind of relationship was what she needed.

They drove into a tunnel that plunged directly through a mountain. In the low light, Lacy experienced a heady sense of freedom. She could just be herself this weekend and enjoy his presence.

In a moment of private exultation, she raised their clasped hands to her lips and planted a series of kisses across his knuckles. "Fine with me, Holt. We'll just keep it to the immediate."

When they emerged from the tunnel, Holt caught a glimmer of new light in Lacy's eyes. Whatever he'd said must have been right. He wouldn't examine it or question it, though. He'd just be grateful. Holt hadn't seen her look so relaxed in his company since they'd first met. He wanted to think he was responsible for making her happy. It was definitely a nice feeling.

When they arrived at the tiny mountain town of Cloudcroft, he drove directly to the lodge. Parking in front of the historic, almost century-old hotel, he switched off the engine and hesitated before moving.

"What's wrong, Holt?"

He took a deep breath and gazed straight ahead. "One room or two, Lacy? You decide."

"How many rooms did you reserve?" she asked in a practical tone.

"Two."

"Well, maybe—" she paused and swallowed hard "—maybe you should cancel one."

"Only if you, ah, want it this way. No pressure, Lacy."

"You don't care?"

He looked at her. She was smiling faintly. His arm went around the back of the seat, his fingertips barely touching her shoulder. "Oh yes, I care like crazy. I want you completely, Lacy. But I won't ruin what we already have by rushing you into a sexual situation."

"What if I rush you?" Her grin was spontaneous and teasing. "I think we should stay together."

His arm dropped to circle her shoulders, and he pulled her closer to him as he kissed her. His lips crushed hers in a moment of rugged desire. The pent-up passion he felt for her rushed forth, and he struggled to contain it and himself.

Hands interlocked, they walked up the steps leading into the Bavarian-style hotel. Lacy savored the crispness of the air, the fresh scent of pines, the pungent smell of mesquite wood smoke, the tautness of anticipation. She had thought about Holt Henderson a lot, even dreamed about him a little. Now, what would it be like to hold him, to have him?

Entering the lodge was like stepping back in time. The giant lobby fireplace was flanked by spread-eagle wolf furs and bearskins. Rebecca's Restaurant featured a beautiful wooden bar once owned by Chicago gangster Al Capone, and the old Red Dog Saloon had miners' dollar bills pinned to the wall. They checked in, then followed the bellboy up the creaky staircase to their room. Holt again reached for her hand. In that moment, Lacy had the distinct feeling that in spite of the old-fashioned setting, this was a time of forward motion, the beginning of a bright and shining future for the two of them. Oh, how she wanted to believe her feeling!

As the bellboy ushered them in, Lacy's gaze swept the quaint room, with its flocked red wallpaper and old-fashioned furniture. An oak washstand held a hand-painted water pitcher and bowl. A large window draped with a silk valance and layered sheer curtains framed a fabulous view of the multihued mountainside. Finally, her eyes moved to the bed, with its ornate iron frame. The bed where they'd lie soon....

With a quick sweep, Lacy flopped her suitcase onto the leather-strapped rack and feverishly began to unpack. Why was she nervous? It wasn't as if this was the first time *ever*. And this was a moment she'd anticipated with a certain degree of eagerness. Well, she told herself, this was her first time with Holt. And she wanted it to be good. And yes, she was as nervous as a caged cat. She couldn't help it.

Holt tipped the bellboy and closed the door. They were completely alone now. He dropped his suitcase near the bed and walked to the window. Everything was silent. She could feel the tension mounting between them. Her hands moved faster, needing to be busy. What should she say? Who would make the first move?

"Lacy. Come over here."

She looked up, unconsciously holding her breath.

"This view is fabulous. You can see the tunnel we came through, as well as the mountains."

Releasing her breath slowly, she joined him. He placed his hand lightly on her shoulder, and they stood gazing out the window for a tight minute.

"Know what I'd like to do?"

"I can guess."

"Oh?" He drew back a little. "What?"

She nodded toward the bed.

"Wrong, Mayor."

She giggled, knowing full well she wasn't far wrong. "You're hungry?"

"No. The lunch we had on the way will hold me." He pulled her closer and took a step toward the window. "I'd like to take a hike right over there, where the red oaks mingle with the gold aspens."

"You serious?"

"Never more. Let's get outside for a little while." He turned her in his arms and slid his hands around her waist. "It'll loosen the kinks of driving and relieve the tension in here."

She lifted her eyes apologetically. "I'm sorry."

"Don't worry about it. I feel it, too. It's perfectly natural." He kissed her lightly. "We'll go commune with nature and see what happens."

"You are absolutely amazing, Holt Henderson. You finally get me alone, in a romantic room that reeks of history, with the bed right there—" she grinned "—and you want to take a hike."

"Are you trying to persuade me to stay? Wouldn't take much. Don't think for a minute that I don't want you." He bent and whispered into her ear. "I could take you right now, Lacy. I could stretch you out on that bed and strip every piece of clothing from that beautiful body of yours and ravage you with great pleasure...." He nibbled sensuously at her earlobe.

She giggled nervously, wondering for a moment if he would forget the walk in the woods and take her, here and now. "Savagery isn't exactly your style, Holt."

"And I know it will do nothing for our relationship. I'd rather love you passionately and feel your willing response. I want you to know the same intensity, the same hard desire I'm feeling. It should be shared to really be good."

Lacy felt a rush of desire as she listened to his erotic confessions. "Okay, nature boy, let's go commune with the trees."

They clambered down the creaky stairs, laughing and touching and pausing once for a brief kiss and again for a longer one. It only took a few minutes to drive to the perfect remote spot for a hike in the woods.

The afternoon sun filtered golden and bright through the autumn foliage. A breeze rustled the leaves and tossed a few clouds along the mountaintops. In the far distance, thunder rumbled faintly. But Holt and Lacy didn't notice. They only had eyes and ears for each other.

Their footsteps were soft crunches on a thick forest carpet. They climbed a steep hill, with Holt leading and Lacy following. She watched his long legs stride ahead of her, his strong muscles bunching to push him ever upward. He didn't seem to have any trouble with his knees, while hers already felt like rubber. Near the top, she halted and braced one hand on a sycamore trunk. "Holt," she panted. "Wait up a minute—"

"High altitude getting to you?" He returned to her spot.

"Must be. I feel like I can't get enough oxygen. Either that, or I must be in pretty bad shape," she said, puffing. She placed her palm to her rib cage and took several deep breaths.

"We're probably moving too fast." Holt's gaze traveled to her hand and took in the gentle swells of her breasts above her flat stomach. His candid opinion was that she was in great shape, but he kept it to himself. It took great effort not to touch her soft, heaving breasts.

"I'm hot," she complained, running her hand under the weight of her hair. "I should have put my hair up." She piled it on her head and held it with her hand.

Holt found the action too much. He reached out, placing his hand over hers. His fingers slid down to curl around her heated neck. His gaze locked with hers. "Lacy...." Gently he pulled her closer and closer until his mouth touched hers. The kiss was sweet and seductive, his lips softly sipping at hers. "We could," he murmured between sips, "take our clothes off and ... run naked through the woods."

"Communing with nature?"

"Why not?"

Her hand crept beneath his sweater to touch the lattice of heated muscles along his spine. "Take it off, Holt," she murmured between her own array of responsive kisses.

Without hesitation, he pulled the sweater over his head and tossed it onto the ground. "How's that?"

Her gaze traveled over the width and breadth of his chest. The broad expanse was covered with crisp, dark curls that dipped and curved on the natural waves of well-defined muscles. He was exceedingly masculine, and she felt overwhelmed by his size, which seemed larger right now as he stood before her bare chested. She nodded her approval. "Nice. Very nice."

"Now you." He gestured. "Your sweater."

"Me?" She laughed.

"Yes, Lacy. You."

"Not out here."

"I did."

"I know, but you—" She stepped back. "You're different."

"Let's compare." He moved forward and smiled down at her. One of his knees touched hers. "Come on, Lacy. Take it off."

She grinned at him. She knew she was caught and that Holt had no intention of letting her off the hook. But she couldn't give in too easily. That would take away some of the fun. "Now, Holt...." She stepped back again and halted against a tree. She pressed her back flat against it. "Someone might see."

"Out here?" He looked around mockingly. "There isn't a soul in sight. Maybe a squirrel. Or a wild coyote. But that's all. Come on. Do it for me."

He loomed close and, unable to resist, she reached out with one hand and touched him. With feathery fingertips, she caressed his chest.

He quivered beneath her light strokes, yearning for more. More touching, more caressing, more of her....

There was only one way. He gathered the bottom edge of her sweater and worked it over her head, then tossed it onto the ground with his.

She didn't object.

Holt smiled at the pert way her breasts tented the silky pink teddy she wore. His eyes couldn't disguise his blatant male admiration as he stroked the embroidered silk. Her breasts were soft and pliable. Their tips were firm caps. "Lovely. Oh God, Lacy, you feel—"

Before either of them knew what was happening, a fast, clumsy clinch became a vigorous embrace. He couldn't press her body close enough; she couldn't get enough of his kisses. Weak-kneed with desire, she sank, taking him with her.

Kneeling, with her almost-limp form clutched to the aroused juncture of his thighs, his hands worked beneath her teddy and spread across her back. Her skin was like satin over a slender frame and oh, so inviting. He thought he'd die if he couldn't touch her, all of her.

Breathless and barely able to contain himself, Holt lowered her to the sweaters he'd dropped to the ground. He straddled her without placing any weight on her. "Oh, Lacy, I want you. You know I do."

She looked up at him, passion darkening her blue eyes. Seductively her hands climbed his shoulders, and she pulled him down to her, pressing his bare chest to her silk-and-lace breast. "I want you, too, Holt. You are the most exciting man I've ever known," she murmured in a whisper.

"You're fabulous." He scooted the teddy down to her waist and feasted his eyes on the sight of her exposed breasts. "And so sexy." He quickly removed her jeans and the exquisite teddy.

Lacy boldly placed her hand on his crotch, jerking the snap on his jeans open. With agonizing slowness, she lowered the zipper. Reaching inside his jeans, she touched his fullness, rubbing gently at first, then with a firmer stroke. "Communing with nature is such fun."

Holt made an unintelligible noise as he pulled her closer, manipulating her body to align with his. "My beautiful, beautiful Lacy." He slid his hands under her hips and lifted her against him. She arched eagerly for the pressure he provided until she could feel the mushrooming of desire within her own body. She longed for the strength of his manhood, wanted to know the fulfillment of being one with Holt.

Lacy was no longer the self-sufficient mayor, no longer the rejected woman, no longer the woman who didn't need a man. Right now she was a woman who needed this particular man. She craved Holt with a passion she'd denied too long. He obviously needed her, and she found that extremely rewarding.

"Holt, I want you—" She gasped as he pressed hard against her.

He moved into the V of her legs. "Lacy—"

"Yes. . . ." With a low moan, she began gyrating against the strength of him, seeking his sex and the ultimate satisfaction she knew they could create together. She arched her back and began to rock. "Your jeans. . . ." she murmured against his kiss. In the next moment, the whole earth seemed to quake and enfold them. Lacy reveled in this ecstasy and wanted it to last forever.

But a loud rumble brought her fantasy to a halt. It was real thunder she was hearing, not the magic of their passion.

Minutes—maybe aeons—passed before Lacy fully realized where their wild embrace was leading. They had to stop. They were in the middle of the woods, for Pete's sake! "No, Holt—"

He was breathing hard, fumbling with his jeans.

She grabbed his hands and squeezed. "Wait!" She heard another rumble. She could smell it in the air. Rain! It would be cold and wet. They had to do something. Quick! "Holt . . . Holt, listen. It's . . . it's going to storm. We have to get out of here!"

At that moment, a crash of thunder punctuated her declaration, and Holt raised his head with a start. "What the—"

"We . . . we'd better be going. I'd hate to get caught like this."

He nodded silently and, with a look of considerable anguish, helped her to her feet.

She gazed into his passion-dark eyes. "I'm sorry, Holt."

"It's okay. This wasn't the way I'd planned it, anyway. The middle of the woods isn't very romantic."

"With you, it is."

He kissed her, then handed Lacy her jeans. As she stepped into them, the rain started. They threw on the rest of their clothes as big, cold splats of water pelted their bodies with a chilling force. By the time they ran, stumbling and scooting down the hill to the car, they were soaked and covered with slick, slimy mud. Holt threw open the Jeep door for Lacy.

She halted and drew back, her hand on one breast. "Wait!"

"What?"

"I forgot my teddy! It's somewhere up there. Oh, please—" She looked up at him, rain drenching her face.

"Let it go!"

"I can't leave it." She looked appealingly at him. "It's like littering."

" 'Littering'!" He threw his head back and laughed. "Some destitute wild animal will get it and take it back to a barren nest for additional warmth for the winter."

She shook her head. "I'll go get it." Lacy started back up the hill, sliding to her knees before she took two steps.

Holt grabbed her, picked her up in his arms and carried her into the shelter of the Jeep with him. "We'll come back and get it tomorrow, Lacy." He swiped the moisture from his face. "It's too risky to go back now. Remember when you and your friends' cars got stuck in the gumbo mud? Well, that'll happen to you, my little redheaded darling! This place is quickly getting soggy. And I can't take a chance on your getting stuck." He kissed her wet cheek. "I don't know anyone around with a snowplow!"

She giggled and pushed playfully on his arm. "I can't believe I forgot to put it on!"

"No one will ever know." He hugged her hard. "Did I ever tell you that you're gorgeous when you're filthy?"

"So are you!"

"We're two of a kind. I don't know when I've ever had this much fun in the mud."

"Me either. Oh, Holt, it's been ages since I've had this much fun—period!" She absorbed his embrace and pressed her head to his chest. "Maybe never." And she meant it.

7

"I DIDN'T KNOW it was that much fun to play in the mud," Lacy said with a giggle as they stepped inside the large foyer of the lodge.

"Now I see why mud wrestlers love it."

Just as Lacy and Holt dodged into the hall, a well-dressed couple appeared at the head of the stairs. They stared, seemingly appalled at the muddy and bedraggled pair.

Lacy and Holt stood back to allow the couple room to descend the stairs.

"How-do," Holt said with a friendly smile. He doffed an imaginary hat to the lady when she cast a curious glance at them. "The rainstorm caught us...unawares."

He nuzzled Lacy's earlobe with a little chuckle.

The woman's eyes widened as her imagination obviously kicked into gear.

"We were just communing with nature," Holt added with a sassy grin.

The very proper woman sniffed and clutched her mate's arm as they sailed away, noses in the air.

Holt ushered Lacy toward the stairs. "Should I tell her we got caught with our pants down?"

"Holt! Hush!"

He'd never felt so rambunctious and daring. No one mattered to him right now except Lacy. And it was a wonderful, carefree feeling.

"Let's hurry," Lacy begged, pulling on Holt's arm. "Before they have us thrown out! We do look pretty terrible."

He patted her bottom as they raced upstairs. "They'd really be shocked if they knew you had on no underwear."

"Shh! You said you wouldn't tell!"

"And that you're the dutiful mayor of a fine, upstanding town." He continued to taunt her in a loud whisper as they approached their floor. "And that I almost seduced you in the woods. Or was it the other way around?"

"Holt!"

"I suppose it's debatable as to who seduced whom."

Lacy clamped her hand firmly on his mouth and muttered, "Another word and I'll have you tossed in the local jail for disturbing the peace, buster!"

"I love it when you try to throw your weight around, Mayor." They stopped in the hall by their room, and Holt began fumbling in his jeans pocket for the key.

"Hurry!" Lacy encouraged, glancing to see if anyone else was around. She didn't want to be caught again.

"What's the big rush now that we're inside?" He stopped searching for the key and wrapped his arms around her. He traced a finger down her muddy cheek. "Isn't this stuff supposed to be good for your complexion? I think you look wonderful with mud on your face. But then, you look wonderful any way."

"Holt! The key!" She twisted in his arms and slipped her hand into his pocket to search for the key herself. She felt the tautness of his thigh and the intimacy of his maleness.

"I *like* this!"

Her hand was hot and perspiring by the time she touched the flat little key and quickly extracted it. "We are going inside before another person sees us like this."

"Now, Mayor. Don't worry about your good name. I'll give them our alias. Mr. and Mrs. Harry Finkle-stein."

"Yeah, sure." She opened the door and dashed inside.

Once in the privacy of their room, Holt took her in his arms. "I won't embarrass you, Mayor. Ever."

"What name did you give at the desk?"

"Mr. and Mrs. Harry Jones."

"'Mr. and Mrs.'?"

"You don't mind, do you? I wanted it to look legitimate and not cast any suspicion on the honorable mayor."

"No, it's fine." She shrugged off the aversion she had to the idea of marriage, even when it was fictitious. This was different. He'd done it for her. "As long as we're pretending."

"'Pretending'?"

She tossed her head and laughed lightly. "All of this is pretending, isn't it? Just for fun?"

"This isn't pretending, Lacy. This is the real thing." He lowered his head and kissed her passionately, letting his lips seduce and play with hers.

She succumbed to the beauty of the moment, the glory of the feelings Holt brought out in her. In his arms, caught in his kisses, Lacy became a sensuous, loving woman. It was a part of her that she'd thought was lost or hidden or maybe even gone forever.

When he finally lifted his head, she was clinging to his shoulders, leaning on his welcome strength and delighting in her responses. Whether they were pretending or not, she was enjoying this time with him. She stroked the front of his sweater, purposely lingering on his buttonlike nipples in the process. "Don't you think we should get out of these muddy clothes?" Her voice was soft and sexy.

"Indeed I do."

"And take a shower?" She slipped from his arms, and with a seductive toss of her red curls, headed for the bathroom, stripping as she went.

"Indeed, yes!" He followed her, pulling the muddy sweater over his head.

"My hair! It's even in my hair!" Lacy wailed as she inspected her image in the mirror.

Holt watched as she slithered out of her jeans. She was so damned sexy that every move she made created a distinct tightening in the lower regions of his anatomy. He admired her pale, bare bottom and proceeded to strip off his wet jeans, too. "Want me to wash it?"

She gazed slyly over her bare shoulder as she turned on the taps. "My hair?"

"Sure. Or anything else you want washed."

She turned to face him with a smile. "My hair." She leaned forward and cupped his face with her hands. "My hair first. Then . . ." She shrugged and kissed his lips quickly.

Holt ached with a new, hard desire. "Anything you want, Lacy."

"You," she murmured, and adjusted the water, then stepped under the warm shower spray. Eagerly Holt joined her.

Lacy stood facing him, letting the hot spray soak her red hair and turn it a shade darker. The water dripped from her hair and cascaded down her body. She leaned her head back and closed her eyes. A stream of water made its way down her face, ambling across her cheeks and dripping off her chin.

Holt took a shaky breath and bent to lick that moist trail. Her skin was like silk. She was so beautiful, and oh, how he wanted her. Again.

"My hair," she whispered hoarsely, not opening her eyes. She reached out and held on to his chest for balance.

Holt knew that if she had touched him any lower, he couldn't have contained himself. But she didn't. And he held back. For now.

He willed himself to use some self-control as he poured shampoo into one hand, then rubbed it into her hair. The liquid burst into rainbow-colored foam on her dark red curls. "This reminds me of the soap bubbles we played with as kids. Remember those bottles of soap that made bubbles when you blew on the little plastic thingy?"

"Umm...." She smiled, her eyes still closed. "Remember soap pipes?"

"Um-hmm." He spread his fingers around her scalp, cupping her head, massaging firmly.

"My sister and I got sick on bubble pipes once when we pretended to be smoking like Grandpa." She rolled her head back loosely in his hands. "Oooh... that's nice."

"How did you get sick on a bubble pipe?" He watched her cherry lips as she smiled and talked. Undoubtedly she had the most alluring lips he'd ever seen. Ever kissed. He wanted to kiss those lips again.

She chuckled. "We inhaled the bubbles!"

He placed his lips on hers and murmured, "I'd like to inhale *you* right now." The erotic play had worked its magic on Holt, and he had just about reached his max-

imum endurance. His arms circled her slick, sexy form,
and he hauled her against his own hot, aroused body.
His chest and shoulders presented a fortress to which
she clung as he pressed his male strength against her.
The two of them wriggled beneath the warm shower,
kissing, writhing together, letting the natural force of
the water rinse her hair and bind them into passion.

She raised her arms to comb her fingers through her
hair and make sure it was rinsed thoroughly, and Holt
ran his large, soapy hands over her enticing body. She
was like a porcelain goddess in his grasp. Her breasts
were pert and uplifted by the stretch of her arms. He
relished the way they felt in his hands, the pliancy of
their undersides, the sharpness of her nipples as they
jutted out to meet him. He bent to kiss each one, suckling the moist, strawberry tips until they were large and
pouting.

Lacy, her eyes still closed, relished the sensations
surging through her body. The feeling of his aroused
maleness, his erotic touch, the warm shower beating
down on them all combined to carry her away to a fantastic ecstasy. It was almost like a dream, except the
feelings were real.

She'd never known loving could be like this. Holt was
so agreeable, so eager to please, so much fun. She felt
as if he were there just for her pleasure, her delight, her
sexual renewal. And she loved the feeling of being
pampered, of being the complete center of his attention, of his tender but powerful loving. After so many
years of suffering rejection and feeling the need to per-
form and produce, she relished being tempted and
spoiled and sought after in a sexy game of delights.

She arched her back, thrusting her breasts more fully
into the curve of his hands and the warmth of his

mouth. She was thrilled by the way his palms completely covered her breasts and the knowledge that he dominated her body with his. It excited her beyond belief. And it brought her pleasure beyond her wildest dreams.

His palms slid to the sensitive sides of her breasts while his thumbs stroked her taut nipples. She reached out to brace herself by holding his shoulders.

As he straightened, his ardent hands traced her figure, gliding down her waist and hips. Then he spread his fingers across each buttock and pressed her to him. She moved willingly with him.

His sex was hot and aroused against her lower belly. She moaned softly into his kiss and rocked her hips at his urging. His tongue sought the inner recesses of her mouth, tasting and teasing with an erotic pulsating motion. She responded with a playful action of her tongue against his.

Lacy was completely wrapped in Holt's warmth and passion. She felt very secure with him and wanted to press him into her deepest part. Even though it had been little more than an hour since they'd engaged in that wildly erotic sojourn in the woods, she was aroused again. And this time, she was perhaps more eager, more overwhelmed with desire than the last. Mere thoughts of him excited her.

Is this the way it would be with Holt? Would each time she gave herself to him be better, wilder than before? At the moment she felt an inner urging for him that was beyond her control. She wanted to be captured by his strength. She wanted him to take her, wanted him in her—fully and completely and with all his force. It was crazy—and wonderful! It was fun, something she hadn't considered sex to be in many years. Sex had been a requirement. And it required a result. But not now. Not with Holt.

"Please...." she murmured between kisses. "Holt, take me now."

"Here?" His hands spread over her back and stroked downward.

"Yes." She dropped her kisses to his chest, laving each wet, hard nipple with her tongue. Then, daringly, she moved lower on his anatomy.

His stomach grew taut as her wild kisses spread over him. "Lacy, are you prepared? Otherwise, I'll get—"

"I'm fine." She followed the dark hair trail, her lips seeking and teasing his hardness. Her slick hands slid erotically over him, touching him everywhere, enticing him into a fevered heat.

With a low groan, he gathered her to him. Reaching beneath her hips, he lifted her off her feet and braced her against his chest. Instinctively, she clutched his shoulders and hooked her legs around his hips.

She could feel his powerful arousal and, unable to stop, she wriggled against him, letting him know how much she desired and anticipated their union.

He lifted her higher, then lowered her slowly and skillfully until they merged. She opened to him, then grew tight as he filled her. Gripping his shoulders with frantic fingers, she arched back. She felt him burgeoning deep inside her, and a wild array of feelings rippled through her body.

Lacy felt possessed and possessive at the same time. She was aware of sensations yet couldn't help wondering if she was in a dream. She was in charge of the moment, with a certain kind of power over Holt that was especially gratifying to her female instincts. She'd wanted him and he was there for her. The knowledge gave her joy and delight.

She clutched Holt as they came together in an explosive climax, and she continued to hold him, enjoying the moment and hoping it would last forever.

But, of course, it couldn't. Finally, he lowered her to her feet, and, with the warm water still spraying their sensitive bodies, he tenderly washed her with his hand. Then Holt turned the shower off, wrapped her in a towel and carried her to bed.

His kisses were sweet and loving now, not teasing nor urgent. Together they curled under the quilted cover and dozed. Hunger awoke them a few hours later, and they enjoyed a trout dinner in Rebecca's Restaurant and danced in the Red Dog Saloon. The rain continued through the night, and they slept in each other's arms. Full of peace. Full of contentment.

The next morning, it was still raining when Lacy woke and slipped out of bed. Wrapped in a robe, she stood by the window.

The clouds hung heavy and low, spilling their steady drizzle. A thick fog drifted among the tree trunks and rose to mingle with the misty air. It was eerie but beautiful. Yes, a beautiful morning.

Lacy smiled to herself. She felt strangely like humming. Usually, she hated rainy weather. But this time, for some reason, it was different.

She turned to gaze at Holt, the man who'd loved her so fiercely and held her so securely through the night. The eyelet-edged sheet was pushed to his waist, revealing his broad, hairy chest. The frills looked incongruous next to his dark, obvious masculinity.

He lay on his side, one muscular arm crooked and resting on his hip, the other flung over her pillow. She looked at him longingly, imagining herself lying in his arms.

Her thoughts must have been transferred to him some way, for he stirred and reached for her. Realizing she was gone, Holt turned over to look for her. When he spotted her by the window, his sleepy eyes squinted at her, and he smiled. "Mornin'. What are you doing over there?"

"Watching the rain."

"Is it still raining?" He glanced toward the window.

"Hmm. Looks like no letup."

Yawning, he laced his fingers behind his head. "Do you like to watch the rain?"

"Not usually. At least, not until now. It was always too depressing." She nodded to the scene outside. "But this rain is so beautiful. . . ."

"Well, if you're not having too fabulous a time over there watching the cold rain, I'd like to invite you where it's warm and dry." He patted the empty space beside him. "There's a spot reserved specifically for you, Lacy. This is where you belong on a cool, rainy morning."

She smiled at him. He looked adorable, so ruggedly handsome waiting in that bed for her with his hair disheveled and his chest bare and his blue-gray eyes appealing to her. "Come . . . come to me," they seemed to say. She couldn't resist. She tossed off her robe and slid back into bed beside him, into the nest of his arms.

He kissed her, sweetly, gently. "I'd like to make love to you, Lacy. Slowly and thoroughly, not in a wild rampage that leaves us both crazy."

"I like your wild rampages, Holt," she murmured, and returned his kiss. She made her tongue dance inside his mouth and around the sensitive sides.

He responded with a kiss so strong that it left her breathless. Then, before she could think straight, his lips moved along her chin and neck. He detoured to her earlobe and nibbled the tip, then made his way to her neck and breasts. He kissed the soft mounds, suckling each tight, pink nipple.

She arched upward. "Oh, Holt. You know just how to make me feel . . . the best ever."

"Thinking about you used to drive me crazy. Now, touching you does. I don't want to stop. Ever."

"Then don't."

"Mmm, you tempt me." With one finger, he traced a line down the center of her body. Moist kisses soon followed through the fragrant valley between her breasts, down her tummy, pausing long enough to tease her navel. His lips continued their erotic journey downward, moving lower, lower, until she could no longer remain still. His actions were strong and relentless, leaving her weak and moaning for more.

She reached up to grip her pillow as he moved between her legs. She writhed with the pleasure and lost herself in the delight of his passionate inducement. Fulfillment was only moments away, and she wanted him with a demanding desire. Just as she cried out, he moved over her, heart to heart, belly to belly.

"Lacy—"

"Yes, come to me." Her voice was a breathless gasp, and she couldn't lie still. She yearned for him so intently that she felt a deep aching and the urge to force him quickly into her. Then his hard, probing flesh met hers. She was hot—burning—as she moved to make it easier for them, to make it happen.

"Be still," he whispered as he entered her.

"I can't," she protested. "I don't want to. I want you. Oh Holt—" Her movement became frantic and fast. She rocked hard beneath him until she felt climactic ripples surging through her entire body. Crying out, she bit his shoulder softly to muffle herself.

He felt the pain and pressed harder until he filled her completely. Her soft moans of pleasure reassured him that she was enjoying this as much as he. He knew, as she arched high, that he had been able to give her the ultimate pleasure and satisfaction. Even as he fought to control his own urges, he reveled in knowing that she had peaked.

He waited patiently until she lay peacefully beneath him before attempting to show her the pleasure again. He slid his hand between them and stroked her most sensitive spot gently.

"Holt . . . again?"

"Want to?" He could feel her beginning to respond.

"Yes."

To Lacy's delight and surprise, her passion reawakened and quickly grew to new heights. The feelings swelling inside her were different this time, more intense, less physical, deeper than she'd ever known. She just wanted to tuck him inside and hold him there indefinitely.

This time, he rode vigorously to the crest of emotion and beyond, taking her with him. Time stood still as their frenzied motion peaked. And when they were sated, they collapsed together, enfolded in each other's arms for a long, long time.

Finally Holt moved and shifted to his side. "Ah, Lacy, you're wonderful."

"*We* are."

"I confess. Pretty great."

"You don't need to ask how it was for me," she murmured lightly. "I'm afraid everyone in the hotel knows this time." She giggled. "And you know something? I don't care!"

"That's what I like," he said as he rolled away from her and headed for the bathroom. "A woman who enjoys her sex."

"I've never enjoyed it like this," Lacy said as she joined Holt in the bathroom.

"Me, either." Holt was stepping into the shower, and he didn't seem to realize she was dead serious.

After they finished showering, Holt ordered room service. "How does an intimate breakfast sound to you?"

"Great!" Lacy muttered through her toothbrush.

Holt pulled on brief jogging shorts and relaxed on the bed, taking great and obvious pleasure in watching her brush her hair. "You're beautiful, you know."

She gave him a modest smile.

"Lacy, I find it hard to believe that there isn't anyone in your life. You're so—" he paused, groping for the appropriate word "—alluring. No, that isn't enough. You're enticing and smart and fascinating and . . . very sexy. You're everything, and I can't believe you aren't swamped with men."

"I'm too busy. And in case you haven't noticed, there isn't a plethora of available men in Silverton." She grinned devilishly and reached for a nightshirt. She pulled it over her head, then whirled around. Garfield, the cartoon cat, grinned broadly on the shirt's front. "You call this sexy?"

He groaned and slapped his forehead.

"It's comfy." She shrugged hopelessly. "I don't really have the proper attire for a romantic weekend. Guess it's because I don't have many of them." Like none, she thought wryly.

"But you are prepared, aren't you?"

" 'Prepared'?" She brought her body lotion over to the bed and propped one leg beside him. "Want to do the honors?"

"Love to." He began to smear the cream on her smooth, shapely leg. "Lacy, I...uh, didn't see any birth control pills in your stuff. When you said you were protected, I assumed that's what you were taking."

"You looked?"

"Well, it's all spread out on the counter. I didn't pry."

He felt her muscles tighten suddenly. She stiffened all the way down to her toes. He looked up at her.

"You checked on me! Don't you believe me when I say it's okay?" she snapped.

"Yes, of course. I'm just curious."

"Don't worry, Holt. I won't hit you with a surprise paternity suit."

"My God, Lacy! I didn't mean to—"

"I know. Sorry." She moved away from him and, hugging her arms, stood at the window. How could she tell him? What could she say? She should have lied. Then there wouldn't have been this curiosity. These questions. This stress she was experiencing.

"Look, I don't care. It isn't important enough to make you mad. If you say you are, that's enough for me."

She turned slowly to him. "No, Holt, that's not fair to you. I have to be honest. This is something that you should know. I . . ." Her voice lowered. "I can't get pregnant."

He stared. It was not the answer he expected. Yet he'd known something was amiss. She had no birth control paraphernalia of any kind in her toiletries. And she'd been too upset by his simple curiosity. But still, he hadn't figured on this bombshell.

A knock on the door interrupted the tense, silent moment. "Room Service."

Holt took the tray, tipped the busboy and closed the door. He looked back at Lacy, who hadn't moved from her spot by the window. "Well, I guess that answers my question." He poured them each a cup of coffee and brought one over to Lacy. She looked pale and somewhat shaken after her announcement. He caressed her hand as she took the coffee from him. "Let's have a seat and talk about this, Lacy."

She sat in one of the two cushioned armchairs, obviously uncomfortable with the subject. He assembled their breakfast on the table, then settled in the other chair and pulled it so close that their knees touched. He placed his hands around her knees and pressed them together.

"I can tell this is an extremely difficult subject for you, Lacy. And you don't have to talk about it if you don't want to. Remember when I said that I wanted no history to weigh us down? Well, it goes two ways."

"That's sweet of you to say, Holt, but it doesn't matter. My secret's out now." Her hand shook slightly as she lifted the coffee cup to her lips. "You know. And you should know. This . . . this inability is a part of me."

"'Inability'?" He frowned. "Oh, Lacy, I wouldn't call it that. It's just the way you are. Like my bad knees prevent me from doing lots of things I'd like to do."

"Bad knees are nothing like not being able to conceive!"

"True." He nodded slowly. "It's certainly in a different category. Far less emotional. But, a problem just the same. One that keeps me from doing what I want."

"Did anyone ever say your problem was all in your head? Or that if you relax when you do it, that will solve everything?"

"No."

"In fact, *doing it* became an obsession. There were certain times of day when conception was more likely, specific positions, the correct temperature. We worried about all those things. And more. I went to doctors. So did my husband."

"But it was you?"

She nodded miserably. "We did everything recommended by doctors, well-meaning relatives and so-called expert friends of friends who'd call us up and say they heard about our problem. They were about evenly divided on whether we should do it more often or do it less. Our lives revolved around doing it the proper way until I could scream at the thought of—" She covered her face.

"Sounds like a living hell, Lacy."

"It was. I guess that's why I enjoyed spontaneous sex with you so much, Holt. We didn't have to check anything."

He smiled and winked at her in an attempt to soften the mood. "Only one thing. Me."

She wasn't amused. The conversation had dampened her spirits. She'd thought she could do this and not be affected. But it mattered, dammit! It mattered.

Holt poured more coffee for them, then gulped some of his. He turned to her with an earnest expression. "Lacy, I've enjoyed every moment with you. The sex, yes. But also the fun. The conversations. Getting to know you better. Just being with you. Holding you. And none of that has to do with whether you're fertile or not."

"Thank you, Holt. But you don't fully understand." She fiddled with her cup, pushed it around, then picked up a sweet roll. "You can't understand because you have a child."

"Don't condemn me for that."

"I'm not. It's just that I can never have one of my own." She tossed the sweet roll down without taking a bite. "During my marriage, I . . . we became obsessed with the need to have a baby. And when, over the years, I couldn't, I became resigned. It still hurts. But I try to block it out. Sometimes it works."

"Are you also blocking out the hope for happiness with a family of your own?"

She shrugged and laughed dryly. "For now, yes. I've found happiness in my work. Silverton is my baby, and I'm devoted to her. Now that you know what my past has been like and a little of what I am because of this, you can take me home."

"But why? We have a few hours before we need to leave."

"Because I've taken the fun out of everything."

"Not for me." He moved closer. "Not at all." He took her hand and sandwiched it between his. It was cold and clammy. He saw her expression make a quick transition to nonchalance, and it pained him to see her like this. "At the risk of minimizing this condition that you take so seriously, I want you to know that I don't care."

Her eyes opened wide, and she shot him a fierce look.

He lifted her hand to his lips for a kiss. "I don't care what you can do for me. Or what you can produce. What I care about is you, Lacy. You're a beautiful lady and very special to me."

Tears filled her eyes, and she struggled for composure. She'd toughened herself for so many years that to hear this kind of claim from a man, rather than some sort of advice or put-down, touched her heart.

He stood and pulled her to her feet. With all the tenderness in his being, he wrapped her in his arms and enfolded her to his body. He caressed her hair and cupped her head, tenderly pressing it to him.

Lacy laid her head against his chest and thought he was being very nice about this. But she knew the pattern. After they returned home, he would cool their relationship. And she couldn't blame him.

"Lacy," he murmured. "Hasn't anyone ever cared about *you*? Just really cared about you?"

She paused, a little stunned by his question. "I . . . I don't know. I'm sure, at one time. But we lost it along the way to producing the family we both wanted so badly. It gets complicated. And confusing."

"Well, I do. I care about you very much, Lacy. I knew from the first time I saw you that you were special. And now that I've held you in my arms, I'm convinced of it. Furthermore, if you think we're through, you're crazy."

She squeezed her eyes shut, and tears fell on his bare chest and got lost in the mat of curls beneath her head. Now she was more confused than ever. Jason had been angry with her for so long that he didn't even try to stop lashing out. The few other men she'd bothered to tell had been polite, but they reserved the right to back away, which they did as soon as they could.

But Holt was talking about staying on, that they weren't through. It was so confusing.

They finished their breakfast rather quietly. Holt tried to ignite the spark of fun back into their morning, but for Lacy, it was impossible. They decided to head back to Silverton. Their escape weekend was over.

At Holt's suggestion, they stopped at a roadside stand to buy green chiles, a New Mexican tradition. He bought her a red chile *ristra*—a string of red chiles to hang outside her door for good luck and prosperity. The gesture seemed to perk Lacy somewhat, but Holt could see by her eyes that the fun they'd shared was gone.

When they arrived back in Silverton shortly after dark, the flashing red lights of a police car caught their attention.

"What's going on?" Lacy craned her neck. "Would you drive over there, please, Holt?"

"Can't you ever stop being mayor, Mayor? Let the police handle it."

"Looks like it's in the historic district."

"It *is!*" Holt immediately wheeled the Jeep toward the old section. He pulled behind the deputy's car, which was parked directly in front of Holt's renovation project, the Sonoran adobe.

Lacy hopped out quickly. "What is it, Alejandro?" she asked the officer.

"Vandals, Mayor."

"Vandals!"

"Yep. But we caught them." He gestured to his car, where three figures huddled in the back seat.

Lacy leaned over and peered inside. "Roman!"

8

ROMAN TURNED his sullen face away from her, and Lacy could see that he was embarrassed. A wire mesh over the car windows and between the front and back seats reminded her that he and his accomplices were locked in. She straightened and gazed with dismay from Alejandro Bayz, the deputy, to Holt.

"Roman?" Holt's expression was one of pure disgust. "The one who helped me move?"

Lacy nodded.

"How could he?"

"You know one of them?" Deputy Bayz asked.

"Sort of," she said. "What did they do?"

"You don't want to know."

Of course she did. Deputy Bayz accompanied them inside the building with a flashlight. Trash was strewn on the floor. Bold, black-lettered graffiti was spray painted on the walls.

Holt couldn't contain his anger. "This is great! Just damn great! The whole place is a wreck! What a filthy mess! What's that smell?"

"They, uh, put a burro in one of the back rooms."

Lacy gasped aloud.

"Where?" Holt started into the dark part of the building, but Lacy grabbed his arm.

"Holt, there's no use. We've seen enough. Please, come on. We'll let the police handle this. There isn't anything we can do tonight, anyway."

Reluctantly he agreed. Viewing more would only get him more upset. Anyway, Lacy was right. For now, there was nothing he could do. He raved all the way to her house. "I just can't believe this. Dammit, all our work for nothing."

She reached out and squeezed his hand. "I know. I'm sorry, Holt."

"I don't know when I've been so angry." He jerked the Jeep to a halt in front of her house. "For me, yes. But also for all those people who helped last Saturday. This is a town project. They want it to succeed enough to contribute their free time. They've shown their support, and I'm sure other groups had planned to help in the future. But now this travesty negates everything we've done. Who'll want to waste their effort working with me now?"

Lacy nodded sympathetically. She wanted to console him, to reach out to him as he had to her when she poured out her heart about not being able to have a baby. Yet he didn't want consoling. He needed to vent his anger and contempt at the acts of vandalism toward his work project. He needed this private explosion. She understood. She only hoped he wouldn't consider his work futile and decide it was time to move on.

"Don't they have any respect for someone else's property? Someone else's work?"

"Apparently not." She sighed.

"I want vengeance! I want to make those devils suffer for this!"

"Now, Holt, take it easy."

"It's hard when all your work has been destroyed."

"Who knows why in the world they would do such a thing?"

"And who cares? They should learn responsibility." He shook his fist in the air. "I'd just like fifteen minutes with them, to give them a piece of my mind. No, better yet, I'd like to see them clean up the whole damn place and put it back exactly as it was before this destruction."

"Not such a bad idea. Would you like to come in for some chamomile tea and discuss it?"

"No, I'd better go and pick up Alita." He gazed at her in the darkness. "I wouldn't hurt anyone, Lacy. Surely you know me better than that by now. All this has been empty talk. I'm just so damned mad."

"I know. I understand. Believe me, they'll pay."

Holt carried in the heavy string of fresh chiles. She followed with her suitcase. They stood in the doorway, suddenly quiet.

"What a way to end our dream weekend," he said finally.

"With a nightmare."

"But the time we spent together, Lacy, was the most special I can ever remember." He took her in his arms and kissed her, his lips warm and wonderful on hers, conveying the strength of his passion. "When I feel you close, I forget everything, Lacy. And nothing else is important but us. Nothing."

"Not even the vandalism."

"Especially not that. Not even your infertility. Just you and me."

She wanted so desperately to believe him. "When you kiss me like that, I lose myself, too. It's a nice feeling, Holt. Thank you for being so wonderful about all this." She didn't dare admit, even to herself, just how wonderful she felt in his arms.

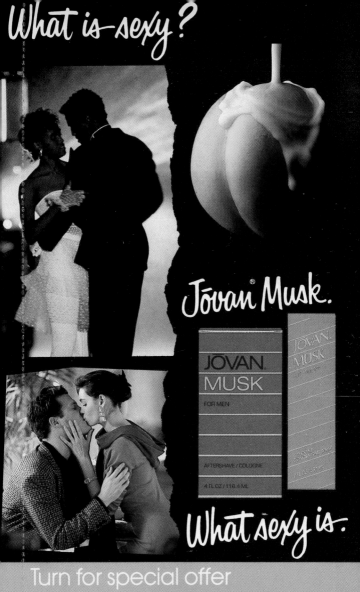

Jōvan® Musk for Women.
What sexy is.
Tear Here

Jōvan® Musk for Women

TO THE RETAILER: For each coupon you accept from the customer at time of purchase of any Jōvan Musk for Women item, Jōvan will pay you $1.00 plus 8¢ handling if terms of offer have been complied with by you and the consumer. Presentation for redemption without such compliance constitutes fraud. Payment will be made only to retailers stocking these products. Invoices proving purchase of sufficient stock to cover coupons presented for redemption must be shown upon request. Coupons may not be assigned or transferred. Any sales tax must be paid by the consumer. Offer good only in the U.S.A. and void where prohibited, licensed, taxed or restricted by law. Cash value 1/20 of 1¢. Unauthorized reproduction of this coupon is prohibited. For payment, mail coupon to Jōvan, Inc., P.O. Box 14851, Chicago, Illinois 60614. Offer expires 12/31/90. **Consumer Note:** Limit one coupon per purchase of any Jōvan Musk for Women item. **Consumer must complete information below to redeem coupon. This information will be kept confidential.**

NAME_____

ADDRESS_____

CITY_____ STATE_____ ZIP_____

HW

5 35017 12376

SAVE
$1.00

MANUFACTURER'S COUPON
EXPIRES 12/31/90

HM

5 35017 12276

Jōvan® Musk for Men

TO THE RETAILER: For each coupon you accept from the customer at time of purchase of any Jōvan Musk for Men item, Jōvan will pay you $1.00 plus 8¢ handling if terms of offer have been complied with by you and the consumer. Presentation for redemption without such compliance constitutes fraud. Payment will be made only to retailers stocking these products. Invoices proving purchase of sufficient stock to cover coupons presented for redemption must be shown upon request. Coupons may not be assigned or transferred. Any sales tax must be paid by the consumer. Offer good only in the U.S.A. and void where prohibited, licensed, taxed or restricted by law. Cash value 1/20 of 1¢. Unauthorized reproduction of this coupon is prohibited. For payment, mail coupon to Jōvan, Inc., P.O. Box 14851, Chicago, Illinois 60614. Offer expires 12/31/90. **Consumer Note:** Limit one coupon per purchase of any Jōvan Musk for Men item. **Consumer must complete information below to redeem coupon. This information will be kept confidential.**

NAME_____

ADDRESS_____

CITY_____ STATE_____ ZIP_____

Jōvan® Musk for Men.
What sexy is.
Tear Here

"No matter what you think, Lacy, it isn't over between us. You won't get rid of me that easily. I'll be back soon. In fact, we should roast those chiles tomorrow night."

"No, you don't have to—"

He hushed her with another breathtaking kiss. "I don't *have* to do anything. But the fact remains that those chiles must be roasted so they'll peel easily. We'll do it together."

"Holt, I don't think we should—"

"You aren't going to start that mayor stuff again, are you, Mayor?" He kissed her nose. "You may be my boss, but you don't direct my off-duty activities. You see, I've found this fabulous redhead, and I'm crazy about her. You wouldn't try to keep us apart, would you, boss?"

"Holt, you're impossible."

"Tomorrow night. Meet you over the hot chiles."

After he left her, Holt wondered if his reaction to her dilemma had been appropriate. Maybe he'd tried to make too light of a very serious subject. He could only be honest with her. He could only show her that he cared for her. More now, after this weekend, than ever.

Even when he picked up Alita and brought her home and listened to her happy, childish chatter, he couldn't forget Lacy's expression. He couldn't shake the sight of those sad blue eyes when she was telling him that she couldn't have children.

"So, Daddy, I want to bring one of my new friends home after school."

"You'll have to ask Mrs. Carson."

"She already said yes."

"Okay, it's fine with me, then."

"Oh, thank you, Daddy!" Alita gave Holt a big hug and kiss on the cheek. "Mrs. Carson is looking for good homes for her baby kittens. And my friend, Hanna, might take one. I might, too."

Holt gave Alita a long, slow glance. "Well, I don't know about that." He wondered if now was the time to visit Annie's Apple Farm and see the dalmatian puppy. He hadn't even mentioned it to Alita. He didn't dare.

"Daddy, I've already picked out my favorite kitten. She's brown and white. Mrs. Carson calls her Calico."

"Hmm? Okay, honey."

"Okay? Can I have her?"

"Huh? No. Did I say that?"

Wisely, Alita switched the subject. "Can Hanna come over for dinner tomorrow?"

"Sure. That's a definite." Holt smiled at his little daughter. After knowing about Lacy's problem, he looked at Alita with a renewed appreciation. Some people never had this opportunity, and he had to acknowledge that he was very lucky, indeed.

Now, if he could only convince Lacy that he felt just as lucky to be with her. He had a monumental task before him, bigger than the vandals' mess in the Sonoran adobe, bigger than renovating the entire historic district. But it was one he would tackle with his whole heart. Lacy Donahue.

THE NEXT MORNING, Lacy waited in her office for Holt. They were to meet and go to the juvenile hearing together. Why did this incident have to happen now? Holt's work on the district had finally progressed to a point where others could see a beginning. Soon they would have the visible proof that she needed to further her quest. She had planned on pointing to their ongoing, successful projects when requesting future funds. By showing their own bootstrap efforts, Lacy felt that she could persuade more entrepreneurs to invest in Silverton's future.

Her deep concern was what this would do to Holt's drive and enthusiasm. Would he quit? Would he become convinced at some point that the town wasn't worth his efforts? Would he decide they didn't appreciate his hard work enough to value it—and him? She shook off the depressing thoughts. Now, more than ever, she wanted him to stay. They needed him.

When Holt arrived, Lacy fixed them a quick cup of soothing chamomile tea. "I wanted to talk to you about something you said last night."

"About us?"

"About the vandals. How you'd like to make them restore the building. Do you mean that?"

"Yes. I would like them to know how much hard work went into the place."

Lacy handed him a steamy cup of tea. Its applelike aroma filled the air. "There's only one way for them to know. That's for them to have hands-on experience."

"You're right."

"But they would need supervision."

"You mean, let them actually clean it up?"

She nodded. "Would you be willing to supervise? Only you know how it really should be."

"Well, I—" he stirred the tea "—I guess so." He exhaled and thought about it for a minute. "Sure. I'll supervise."

"Without losing your cool with them?" She grinned slightly. It was a lot to ask of a man as physical as Holt. Yet she knew he wasn't a violent man. "Why don't we mention it to Judge Corona at the hearing? Maybe she'll agree to a cleanup as their punishment. Realistically, we won't get any actual payment out of them. And putting them in juvenile detention doesn't seem to be the answer in this case. The best punishment is to make them work."

"And maybe they'll learn some appreciation in the process."

"Exactly." Lacy smiled. "You come up with the best solutions, Holt."

"Me? This was your idea."

"But you said it all last night."

"The only thing I remember about last night was your kiss. And how much I missed you."

"I think we'd better go. It's almost time for the hearing." She led the way downstairs, where the courtrooms were located. Outside the magistrate's room, Lacy recognized a local attorney.

"Hello, Lewis. Are you here on this juvenile case?"

"Lacy, good to see you," he responded. "I'm the court-appointed lawyer representing the defendants."

She turned to introduce the two men. "Lewis Orlando, I want you to met Holt Henderson. He's the new construction engineer on the historical renovation."

Lewis shook hands with Holt. "My pleasure. Was this vandalism on one of the buildings you're remodeling?"

Holt nodded. "We'd just cleaned it out, ready for repairs."

Lewis grinned. "I understand they left a burro inside."

"It's awful. What a mess! But Holt has a recommendation that I hope you'll go along with."

"What's that, Lacy?"

"If the judge will agree to probation, we'd like the boys to be assigned to community service so they can be the ones to clean up their own mess. That may give them a better appreciation of the hard work it took to clean out the building and of the value of others' property."

"Sounds reasonable. I'll see if we can swing it, Lacy. But one of the kids is a girl." He nodded to them both. "Nice meeting you, Holt. See you in court."

Lacy glanced quickly at Holt. "A girl?"

Holt shook his head. "What else is new? Well, she made the mess, she can clean as well as the others."

They followed Lewis into the magistrate's room, where the juvenile proceedings would be conducted informally.

As the county attorney presented his case against Candy Hershey, Tony Rios and Roman Barros, Holt leaned close to Lacy's ear and whispered, "Do you know the other two with Roman?"

"Candy's mom died last year, leaving her in charge. Tony's father died a few years ago, and he lives with his mother."

"And who knows for sure about Roman?" Holt furrowed his brow, then turned his attention to Deputy Bayz, who was describing to the judge how he caught the trio.

"Sheriff Meyer instructed me to patrol the historic district more frequently when evidence was found that some vagrants had been sleeping in one of the empty buildings. So, I drove by regularly, according to his instructions. Just after dark last night, I found these kids climbing out of one of the open windows of the old adobe building. One of them had a can of spray paint stuffed in a coat pocket."

Lacy glanced at Holt with a forlorn expression. The evidence was condemning.

Lewis, the youth's court-appointed lawyer, stood and faced Judge Corona for his defense. "Since this is the first offense for all of them, Your Honor, I recommend probation. The mayor suggests that we give the youths some much-needed community service. They can clean up the garbage they distributed in that building and perhaps do a little work to make it better."

Judge Corona nodded and looked over at Lacy. "You agree, Mayor Donahue?"

"Yes, Your Honor. The engineer in charge of the renovation project, Mr. Holt Henderson, has already agreed to supervise their work."

Judge Corona squinted at Holt. "That so, Mr. Henderson?"

Holt took a step forward. "Yes, Your Honor. I'll put them on a work detail after school every day."

The judge nodded, then turned her stern attention to the youths. "You three are to report to Mr. Henderson every afternoon after school for the next month. As your punishment for the crime of vandalism, you are to clean the whole building up, including the, uh, burro's disgusting litter. In addition, you are to carry out whatever other work Mr. Henderson has for you. Do you understand?"

The three nodded in agreement.

When the judge was finished with her warning lecture to the youths, Holt walked forward to meet them. Considering his earlier rage, he felt very calm now. They would be working toward a decent goal. He would see to it. That was enough compensation for him. "You? Roman? How could you do this? Why?"

Roman shuffled his feet and looked down. "Didn't mean no real harm, man." He shrugged and looked up with a grin, which Holt took to be a defense mechanism. "Didn't have nothing else to do, I guess."

"Well, then," Holt responded with a hard edge to his voice, "we won't have to worry about that problem again, because I'm going to see that you stay busy from now on. You'll be so tired when you finish working for me, you'll be glad to go home and fall into bed. Introduce me to your friends."

"This is Tony."

Holt shook hands with a short, slender kid, who looked younger than his alleged sixteen years. "Tony, you and your friends really got into a jam this time."

"Yessir," Tony mumbled.

Roman indicated the other accomplice. "And this is Candy."

Holt shook hands with the dark-haired, chocolate-eyed girl, who would one day be a beauty. "Why did you do it, Candy?"

She shrugged. "It looked like fun."

"Oh. You like to make chaos out of order?"

She glared at him sullenly.

"This cleanup job is going to be harder than any you've ever had. Next time you think destruction is fun, you'll remember this month of hard work, I guarantee." He paused. "Just because you're a girl doesn't mean I'll go easy on you, Candy. You're as responsible for the mess as these guys."

She nodded and looked at Tony, then at Roman.

"See you tomorrow after school at the building. You're going to love it when you're through." Holt walked away and winked solemnly at Lacy.

"You sound like a tough guy," she said, hiding a smile.

"Yeah. I'm real tough," he muttered mockingly, and pushed the door open for her. "See you tonight."

Before she could respond to that, he was gone.

IT WAS NEARLY DARK when Holt and Alita arrived. "Sorry we're so late, but we had to wait for Alita's little friend to leave."

Lacy ushered them inside. She hugged Holt's daughter and took her coat. "Sage needs a buddy tonight, Alita. I made a new catnip toy for him. It's in the kitchen." She smiled as Alita skipped away. Then she turned to Holt. "I'd just about given up on you."

"I would have called if we couldn't make it. Her new little friend is Hanna Barros, younger sister of my constant nemesis, Roman Barros," Holt commented in a low voice. "We had to wait until Roman picked her up on his scooter. Said his aunt couldn't drive. That's a strange situation."

Lacy took his jacket and tried not to pay attention to how his masculine, woodsy scent affected her. "Not so strange around here, Holt. Where would Steve Amado be today if not for Sandy and Jay? Steve's parents are too old and ill to chase after a teenage boy. He'd be on his own a lot, too, just like Roman. He might even have been with Roman and his friends on Sunday night."

"Most likely."

She smiled up at him, her eyes shining with pride. "Now Roman has you to keep an eye on him, Holt. And he has you to look up to as a sort of hero. I think it's going to work out fine."

"It had better." He reached for her hand and held it between his. "You look wonderful tonight, Lacy." His eyes traveled over her face, and his hunger for a kiss was apparent.

She chuckled lightly. "Jeans and shirts bring out my best assets."

"They certainly do." He moved closer and took a deep breath. "And you smell like a garden of roses."

"I'm making herbal tea using rose petals and ginger. Come on out in the kitchen, and I'll show you." She started to take a step, but he held her.

"Is that where Alita and the cat are?"

"Yes."

"Then why don't we stay in here?" He tilted her chin up for a soft kiss. "Alone...."

"Didn't you come over here to roast chiles?"

"Hmm, did I say that?"

"You certainly did. And I'm holding you to it." She tugged on his hand. "Now come on. We have lots of work to do. We can be alone later."

"No, we can't," he muttered as he followed her into her savory kitchen. "We can never be alone between your cat and my— Hi, honey. Having fun?"

"Yes, Daddy. Wouldn't it be fun to have a kitten like this? I'll bet Calico would love to play with Sage."

Lacy stooped so she was level with Alita. "Who's Calico?"

"The kitten Mrs. Carson said I could have."

"Oh, how nice." Lacy looked up at Holt.

Holt smiled tolerantly.

"Mrs. Carson said so." Alita gave her dad a pouting look. "But Daddy didn't."

"Look, we've been over this a dozen times, Alita. Who's going to take care of it when we're both away?"

"I will. And I'll love it!" the little girl said stubbornly.

"Cats are nice pets, Holt," Lacy said, going to the kitchen cabinet where she'd stored the chiles. "Not much work and attention are required."

"We're too busy."

"They're pretty self-sufficient."

"See, Daddy?" Alita folded her arms.

"And completely worthless. They don't *do* anything except look pretty."

"That's nice, don't you think?" She dumped a bag of green chiles into a large pan. "Sometimes you can get one that's something of a watchcat. Like Sage."

"The one who twitches her tail when someone is coming?" He chuckled at her ludicrous analogy.

"She warns me in her own way," Lacy said with a defensive smile.

"Enough about cats, okay?" Holt shifted around the kitchen.

"Okay." Lacy winked at Alita. "On to the chiles! Now, we can roast them in the oven. Or we can put them outside on the grill. I prefer the grill."

"Then, so do I," Holt concurred readily.

Soon Holt and Lacy were busy roasting and freezing the green chiles while Alita watched TV and played with Sage. When their chore was finished, Lacy fixed them all festive bowls of sherbert decorated with sugared violets.

"Never thought I'd be eating flowers dipped in sugar," Holt said as he popped one into his mouth along with a spoonful of sherbert. "And liking it."

"It's whatever you're used to." Lacy curled her legs into the chair and cupped her sherbert bowl in one hand. "If we grew up munching flowers as kids, we'd think no more of eating them than corn on the cob."

"Well, you've exposed one kid to the novel idea of eating flowers. She'll probably remember it always."

"You've made an impact on some kids, too, Holt. Once again you've handled a poor situation quite admirably. I'm really proud to know you."

"Because I eat your flowers without making a fuss?" He lifted a spoonful of sherbert topped with a flower. "Just don't tell the guys, okay? Sugared violets aren't very macho."

Alita giggled and popped a flower into her mouth, too. Then she carried her sherbert into the living room, leaving Holt and Lacy alone again.

"No, because of the way you handled those problem kids this morning. They did a lot of ugly damage to something you'd worked very hard on. And you turned it around."

"Don't you see through my methods?"

"What do you mean?"

He shrugged. "I got myself some free help for the next month."

"I wouldn't consider those three much help. One's a girl, for Pete's sake."

"Girls can work hard. And I've already seen how Roman worked under supervision."

"Without it, though, he just can't seem to manage."

"We all need a little nudge now and then. But don't worry. I won't take my eyes off him."

She shook her head. "You're really amazing. You know, maybe I can incorporate this community action into the special federal grant that I'm applying for for our historic project. We have a strange conglomeration of commitments to list. Annie has come up with a group of ladies who want to open a southwest crafts shop, stock it on consignment and run it on a rotating basis. We think it'll work. Then, I have the Mexican-food restaurant partners for the Sonoran adobe. Now I can add that the buildings will be renovated by juvenile parolees."

"If that doesn't soften the hearts of those who control the purse strings, nothing will!"

"It's for a lot of money, Holt. It would be enough for you to hire a staff. Enough to keep your job secure for at least a year."

"Sounds good." He hesitated. "Is that what you want, Lacy, to keep me around for a year?"

"At least." She smiled, and her eyes lighted with a teasing twinkle. "Or maybe forever."

"Sounds like a 'winning strategy' to me." He covered her hand with his. "I wish we had more time alone."

"Before you have to leave, I'd like to mention an idea that I've been toying with and see what you think." She pushed her empty bowl aside and was suddenly strictly business. "I want to have a dinner at my house and feature some specialty dishes using my herbs and edible flowers. It'll be a unique gourmet dinner, one that I'm hoping will create such a stir, they won't be able to refuse my request."

"'They'? What request?"

"The guests will be a certain group of people from Alamogordo and Albuquerque."

"A certain group of influential people?"

"Right."

"And the request has to do with money?"

She nodded. "Exactly. People with enough money to invest in our dying little town in a program of delayed profits."

"I think that's a great idea, Lacy. Intrigue them with your unusual garden, fill them with good food, then hit them in the pocketbook."

"Holt!" She shook her head at him. "No, no. This is to show them our good intentions, our actions, our needs. And to entice them to join our good and worthy cause. And, as with any sound investment, they'll reap the dividends in the future."

"I think you're a diplomat of the first order."

She quirked one eyebrow. "How do you think I got to be elected mayor? So, will you help me?"

"Of course. What do you want me to do?"

"Be the guest of honor." She grasped his hand. "Now Holt, before you refuse, hear me out. Please."

He listened silently as she rushed forth.

"You know how much hope and faith we all have for the historic district. Also, for your work in it. By the time I could plan and execute an evening such as this, you'll probably have the recent destruction completely cleaned up and the remodeling started. We could take the guests on a tour of the district, featuring the Sonoran adobe." She paused and smiled encouragingly. "Doesn't it sound great, so far?"

"So far, great. Where do I come into the picture?"

"Since you know so much about the history, you could conduct the tour."

"Right."

"And then they could meet you during dinner. That's all. I'll do the rest."

"Coat and tie? Mr. All-Smiles and Nice Guy?"

She squeezed his hand. "Come on, Holt. You know you're our greatest hope, our—"

"'Winning strategy.'"

"Don't say it like that."

"Before we agree to what sounds like a perfectly awful evening, I should tell you that I'm not very political. This kind of event, where you dress up and smile and engage in small talk, is not my kind of function."

"It won't be that difficult. All you have to do is be yourself. Just be there. And act natural. I like you like that. And I'm sure they will, too."

"You know just what to say to influence a guy." He grinned and caressed her hand. "Okay, if that's all you want from me. It *is* for a good cause."

She smiled and leaned over to kiss his cheek. He caught the back of her head and kept her there until he could kiss her lips soundly. "Guess I'm just a sucker for redheads. I'd do anything for you, Lacy. Right now, though, I've got to go. Need to get my little gal in bed. She's awfully quiet in there."

"Thanks for helping with the chiles tonight."

"My pleasure. I'm expecting some fabulous *chili con queso.*"

"You're on. Friday night?"

"I have to wait until Friday night to see you?"

"Unless we have another disaster at work."

"Not again! I couldn't stand another such episode." He stood and pulled Lacy into his arms. One hand touched, then caressed her face. He lifted her chin and kissed her lips softly, teasing them with his tongue.

Lacy felt drawn to him by invisible forces stronger than either of them, and she opened her mouth for the invasion of his tongue. She clung to his shoulders, pressing him to her, wanting more than his kiss.

But he broke away. "Much as I hate to leave, I have to take my daughter home and put her to bed."

Lacy nodded and followed him into the living room. Alita had fallen asleep on the sofa, with Sage curled into the curve of her small body. Holt slid into his jacket, then maneuvered Alita's limp form into her coat. He lifted the child into his arms and whispered good-night to Lacy.

She watched them leave, Alita's head resting on her dad's broad, secure shoulder. The two of them made a sweet sight. What a lucky little girl to have such a strong, reliable father.

Even after Lacy had gone to bed, the image of Holt and his daughter stayed with her. She longed for the feelings, the family and the child she'd never have. And, in the dark of night, the mayor who always managed to wear a tough facade, turned her face to the pillow and cried.

9

"I DON'T UNDERSTAND, HOLT. Two weeks ago, when the vandals were caught, you were furious with them. When they started working for you, you had nothing but problems with them." Lacy lifted one hand and let it drop back to the pile of papers on her desk. "Now you want to hire them and give them a chance."

"When you think about it, Lacy, the confrontations were normal. We had to establish our roles, our positions. They had to learn who were the workers and who was the boss. Believe me, Roman wants to be boss. Once we got that settled, things smoothed out considerably." He shrugged. "This week, they've been working together as a team. With me, not against me."

"You make it sound so simple." She shook her head.

"No, but it's manageable. They need guidance." He sighed. "Actually, they need so much."

"Is the cleanup done?"

"Oh, yes. We're already starting with the remodeling." Holt leaned forward with his elbows on his knees. There was a boyish eagerness in his tone. "You should see them at work, Lacy. Tony and Roman have been helping me with the roofing. It's messy, but they're hard workers and willing to learn. With supervision, they're doing a credible job. And Candy is a natural plasterer. You know, in the old days, the women were the adobe plasterers. They seem to have the skilled hands for it."

"It sounds like you're doing more than supervising their work. You're teaching them skills."

"Now that we're working well together, I'd like to hire them on officially. It would be a shame not to let them continue." He smiled wistfully. "But best of all, Lacy, is their pride in their work. Heck, they're even proud of their cleanup job. I told them I'd ask you to walk through and give it an official inspection. They're anxious for you to see what they've done."

"Well, certainly I'll do that. But hiring... I don't know, Holt."

"It isn't much, but it would give them tremendous incentive and great self-confidence, Lacy. I'm convinced that part of the reason they vandalized the adobe in the first place was that they had nothing better to do."

"And you're willing to give them something to keep their hands busy?"

"You bet. But it's more than busy work. I'm training them in some basic construction techniques. I believe that people can improve their situations by education or training and hard work. What better thing could a town, especially this town, do for its youth than provide job training?"

"You've got a good point, Holt. Actually, for these kids, it's better than providing a pretty park for leisure time. We could be teaching them valuable skills."

"Can't you get the money from some other part of the budget? This is really important."

She tapped her pencil on her desk. "You know, if we branch into job training, I might be able to get a grant that would cover it."

"Actually, we aren't talking about much of a financial layout, Lacy. Minimum wage for two hours a day, five days a week. That's only ten hours' work per week times three." He paused a moment so she could reflect on what he was saying. "I'm sure that these kids need the money from a job, although none of them would ever admit it. But more than that, they need the pride that this particular work will provide. They'll be able to see the results almost instantly, and they'll be a part of the historic renovation. Won't that be great?"

She smiled at him and shook her head. "You're very convincing, Holt. You make some good points. I'm not opposed to it. Tell you what, I'll take it to the town council and see if they'll approve it. We'll need to present an official proposal and financial statement. And I'll develop a budget amendment."

"Thanks, Lacy." He stood. "Now, can you arrange to walk through after three o'clock today when they'll all be there?"

"Of course." She stood and walked around her desk.

He halted and looked at her strangely for a moment, then extended his hand. She smiled and slid her hand into his.

But instead of shaking her hand, he held it firmly and pulled her close. "Ordinarily, Your Honor, I'd settle for a handshake. But this business calls for more." He kissed her quickly on the lips. "See you this afternoon."

Lacy stared at the door after he left. Holt was a steadying force, while at the same time, always catching her off balance with his ideas. He was creative and innovative, the best thing that their town had ever seen. He was a man to look up to, a hero of sorts. And what she so admired about Holt, the man, was his sense of strong values. Honesty. Self-esteem. Pride in a job well-done.

His proposal today to hire the kids was logical. It would help everyone involved, including himself. And yet, she got the feeling that he actually had the kids' best interest at heart. He was doing this for them.

The trouble with having him working here, conferring with him on an almost-daily basis, was that Lacy was drawn to the man, physically and emotionally, with an unreasonable urge. She ran her tongue along her lips, where he'd kissed her. She could taste his masculine flavor, and her senses cried out for more.

Oh, good heavens! What was wrong with her? Quite simply, the man's strong masculinity appealed to her feminine nature. He was darned sexy! He was a man with the kind of personal strength and attributes that she admired. Unfortunately, he was the kind of man she could fall in love with. . . . Maybe she already had.

Lacy sighed heavily, telling herself she had to fight that feeling. Her sense of reason told her it was all wrong.

But her heart wouldn't listen. Her heart responded as if Holt Henderson were exactly right for her.

THE NEXT TWO WEEKS were busy for both Holt and Lacy. His proposal to hire the kids was approved unanimously by the town council. Suddenly he had a work crew. Although they weren't experienced, they were a willing crew who were eager to learn and glad to have the work. Holt found that they were reliable, and soon he was depending on them to do certain jobs.

Lacy tried to keep her distance from him and her mind on the upcoming political dinner she was hostessing. Still, she couldn't help bursting with pride over Holt's accomplishments. His working with the kids was a tremendous gesture and a great success so far. She couldn't wait to show him off. Of course, she didn't let him know that. He'd rebel in a minute. And she'd be stuck with a table full of flowers and no guest of honor.

Preparations for the event were a town effort. Maxine Novak, the school principal, used her calligraphy skills on the handmade invitations. The honored presence of the mayors of Alamogordo and Albuquerque and certain prominent citizens of those cities was requested to a Feast of Flowers with Silverton's mayor. Everyone was so curious about the so-called Feast of Flowers that they didn't dare refuse. Lacy was thrilled when they all accepted, then she really got busy.

On the Saturday of the dinner party, Annie Clayton came early to bring several apple cakes and to help Lacy make dill bread. Jay and Steve Amado hauled in an extra table and moved furniture around so Lacy could seat the twenty guests. Judge Corona brought two treasured lace tablecloths that had been in her family for fifty years. Flowered centerpieces were contributed from businesses in town, and a couple of high school teachers decorated and set the tables.

By the time Holt arrived at the door at four-thirty, the house had been transformed. He peered past her. "Is this the right place?"

Lacy proudly drew him inside, her face flushed with excitement. "Isn't it grand? I can't take the credit. Everybody contributed something."

"But you were the spark, Lacy. You got them rolling." He hooked an arm affectionately around her shoulders and squeezed. "It's going to be a fine evening for flowers. And for Silverton." He kissed her forehead.

She basked in his praise. Oh, he was good for her. She needed his encouragement to fortify her, his energy to strengthen her. No doubt about it, she thrived in his embrace. Caressing the front on his dress shirt, she smiled up at him. "You look very nice, Mr. Henderson, our special guest of honor."

"You're the special one, Lacy." He stroked her cheek with his fingertips, then tilted her head for a kiss. His lips played softly on hers, taking her breath, giving her life.

"I'm lucky to have you here, Holt."

"You sound as if I'm leaving soon. It isn't that easy to get rid of me, Lacy."

"I hope you'll stay forever."

"I'll stick around long enough for the fireworks. They're always at the end of a celebration, aren't they?"

"I don't have any planned for tonight."

He grinned. "Well then, we may have to make our own fireworks."

"Tonight?"

"Mrs. Carson's keeping Alita all night. I wasn't sure how long a Feast of Flowers would take."

"You figured you'd stay afterward?"

"Shh," he murmured, placing a finger on her lips. "I figured you'd need someone to help you clean the kitchen. I'm quite good at it."

A car pulled into the driveway.

"Must be Sandy." Lacy forced herself out of Holt's arms. "She's going to help me serve tonight."

Holt straightened his tie as Lacy opened the door to Sandy's knock.

Later, when the special guests were assembled, Jay Amado drove the school bus that transported them to the historic part of town for their guided tour. As they strolled through the old district, Holt entertained them with hair-raising tales of how Pancho Villa and his gang of rebels had plagued Silverton in the early part of the century. Then he led them into the Sonoran adobe building for a glimpse of the restoration in progress. Lacy distributed small artist's renderings of how the completed project would appear.

The guests were impressed as they were whisked back to Lacy's for rose wine punch and pansied Brie with rice crackers. The cream of dandelion soup brought "oohs" and "aahs" as well as memories of pioneer grandmothers who created the same type of soup in the "old days." The floral salad, featuring nasturtium and chive blossoms on a bed of watercress, was a great success. By the main course of lamb marinated in herbed olive oil, the out-of-town guests were inclined to listen to Lacy's pitch as to how they could profit from efforts to help Silverton survive.

Lacy emphasized that the project was an investment for them as well as Silverton's future. Then she served a dessert of Annie's apple cake topped with crystallized rose petals and tiny, star-shaped, blue borage flowers. By the time they were wiping the last crumbs from their chins, each of the guests had made some sort of commitment to assure that Silverton's historic district would, indeed, be renovated.

After dinner, the crowd started breaking up. Thomas Coy, a banker from Albuquerque, pulled Lacy aside. "I'm very impressed with this evening's display. From the historic district tour to your Feast of Flowers, the evening was superb, Mayor Donahue."

"Thank you, Mr. Coy. Many of our citizens helped put this evening together," she said truthfully. "We all want Silverton to survive."

He nodded. "After what I've seen tonight, so do I."

She looked pleased, expecting his pledge of money or help or both. He was, after all, a banker with access to people who wanted to make investments. "I'm glad."

"I have some specific things in mind for Silverton."

"Oh?"

"The bank that Pancho Villa terrorized particularly interests me. It could be a grand and beautiful building again and make a fine location for another bank. What great publicity we could get. Of course, I can tell that it would take a large sum of money to renovate it."

"That's why we didn't start with that one, Mr. Coy."

"What if I arranged for whatever amount you needed? I have some friends, uh, some venture capitalists, who would be interested in creating another bank here in Silverton."

"Why, that would be great, Mr. Coy."

"I think it could be arranged, then, for a special fund to be set aside."

"I'm sure Mr. Henderson would be very pleased to make the bank building the next project. I suppose we could use another bank in town, if we had the money flow to support it."

"But we might need to alter some of the present circumstances."

"What?"

"Well, uh, you see, I have a son whose construction business in Albuquerque is, uh, sagging under the economy right now. But we can discuss that later. Let's see what we can do about getting this thing rolling first."

Lacy's eyes grew round and large. "Wait a minute. What are you hinting at? That your son do the renovation work on the bank?"

"For his first project, yes. I'm sure you'll find he can handle the other restorations, too. Anyone with the right skills could do it."

"Well, not just anyone." She thought immediately of the impact Holt had made on the community, pulling so many folks into the project in various ways. "Actually, we don't have the funds to hire another builder."

"I understand. But I'm sure something else could be arranged. As I said, we'll discuss the incidentals later." His gaze lifted to someone behind Lacy.

She turned to see Holt standing near the door.

"Your guests want to see you before they leave," he said tightly.

Her eyes met his, and she knew that he'd overheard enough of the conversation to know what had been said. She turned quickly back to Thomas Coy. The man smiled coolly and shook Lacy's hand. Then he turned the same cool smile on Holt and shook his hand, too.

Anger surged through Lacy as she moved away. Obviously Mr. Coy wanted to replace Holt in exchange for the money to renovate the bank. How dare he? Hot with fury, she bit her lip to hide her feelings and made the effort to smile and bid her guests good-night. Now was not the time for a confrontation.

When everyone was gone, Lacy vented her anger to Sandy and Holt as the three of them spent the next hour cleaning the kitchen. Sandy agreed with Lacy. Holt said nothing.

Finally, Lacy sat down wearily. "Thanks for everything, Sandy. We can finish this tomorrow. It's late."

Sandy looked around. "It's in pretty good shape. Jay and Steve will come over in the morning to pick up the table and extra coffeepot."

The more
you love romance . . .
the more
you'll love this offer

FREE!

*Mail this heart today!
(See inside)*

**Join us on a Harlequin Honeymoon
and we'll give you
4 free books
A free bracelet watch
And a free mystery gift**

142 CIH MDVY (U-H-T-09/89)

IT'S A
HARLEQUIN HONEYMOON—
A SWEETHEART
OF A FREE OFFER!
HERE'S WHAT YOU GET:

1. **Four New Harlequin Temptation® Novels— FREE!**
   Take a Harlequin Honeymoon with your four exciting romances—yours FREE from Harlequin Reader Service®. Each of these hot-off-the-press novels brings you the passion and tenderness of today's greatest love stories . . . your free passports to bright new worlds of love and foreign adventure.

2. **A Lovely Bracelet Watch—FREE!**
   You'll love your elegant bracelet watch—this classic LCD quartz watch is a perfect expression of your style and good taste—and it is yours FREE as an added thanks for giving our Reader Service a try.

3. **An Exciting Mystery Bonus—FREE!**
   You'll be thrilled with this surprise gift. It is elegant as well as practical.

4. **Money-Saving Home Delivery!**
   Join Harlequin Reader Service® and enjoy the convenience of previewing four new books every month delivered right to your home. Each book is yours for only $2.39*—26¢ less per book than the cover price. And there is *no* extra charge for postage and handling. Great savings plus total convenience add up to a sweetheart of a deal for you! If you're not completely satisfied, you may cancel at any time, for any reason, simply by sending us a note or shipping statement marked ''cancel'' or by returning any shipment to us at our cost.

5. **Free Insiders' Newsletter**
   It's *heart to heart*®, the indispensible insiders' look at our most popular writers, upcoming books, even comments from readers and much more.

6. **More Surprise Gifts**
   Because our home subscribers are our most valued readers, when you join the Harlequin Reader Service®, we'll be sending you additional free gifts from time to time—as a token of our appreciation.

START YOUR HARLEQUIN HONEYMOON TODAY—JUST
COMPLETE, DETACH AND MAIL YOUR FREE-OFFER CARD

START YOUR
HARLEQUIN HONEYMOON TODAY.
JUST COMPLETE, DETACH AND MAIL YOUR
FREE OFFER CARD.

If offer card is missing, write to: Harlequin Reader Service® 901 Fuhrmann Blvd
P.O. Box 1867 Buffalo NY 14269-1867

BUSINESS REPLY CARD

FIRST CLASS MAIL   PERMIT NO. 717   BUFFALO, NY

POSTAGE WILL BE PAID BY ADDRESSEE

HARLEQUIN READER SERVICE
901 FUHRMANN BLVD
PO BOX 1867
BUFFALO NY 14240-9952

Lacy walked her to the door. "Thanks. I couldn't have done it without you, Sandy."

"You could have pinned an apron on Holt and let him serve the soup and salad." She chuckled, then called, "Good night, Holt."

"G'night Sandy." He stood silently with his hands in his pockets as she drove away.

Lacy turned to him. "You've been awfully quiet about all this, Holt."

He nodded. "Looks like my head's on the block."

"No, it isn't! I would never do what he suggested, Holt. Surely you know that."

"It's politics, Lacy. Done all the time."

She rushed to him and took both his hands in hers. "But not by me. That's not my way. To hurt one so another can make it isn't right in my book."

He shrugged. "We're talking about money for the town, Lacy. Lots of much-needed money. Silverton's future."

"No! Not without you. Silverton has no future without you, Holt."

He looked down at her and smiled. "You're tired, Lacy. It's been a long day. Things will seem different to you tomorrow."

"Not this!"

"Silverton made it before Holt Henderson came along and will certainly do without me in the future."

"Wrong on both counts. How can you say that? Have you forgotten that we are a town without a future? Silverton was slipping into obscurity before you appeared with a promise of hope. That's so important, Holt, for without hope, we have nothing. And the future? We're headed straight for ghost town status."

"Not with you and all the others to work for progress, Lacy."

"You're impossible."

"I'm realistic."

"Well, Mr. Realistic, grab this. Neither Silverton nor I were doing very well before you appeared." She stood on tiptoe and kissed his cheek. "You have become our mainstay, and I won't consider our future without you."

His arm hooked around her waist, and he held her close. For a moment her delicate, lemony fragrance tingled his senses like champagne. "Now this is more like it. How about if I grab you and forget about our argument?"

"Fine with me." She rested both arms on his imposing chest. The physical strength of this tender man always impressed her. His manner, even his power, was subtle and never flaunted. It wasn't necessary. It was just there, as much a part of Holt as his strong gray eyes and slightly ruffled brown hair.

Holt settled her against him. He could feel her heart pounding double beats on his chest and acknowledged his own flesh quickening with each breath of her spicy fragrance. She tilted her head back to look at him, and he saw such happiness in her eyes that he was flooded with an undeniable joy.

"I want to thank you for coming tonight and being the honored guest, Holt. You were an excellent tour guide. No one knows that historic district like you do." She sighed with a rueful smile. "I realize that eating flowers wasn't your favorite way to spend an evening, and I appreciate your pretending."

He kissed her lips gently. They were soft and receptive, with a mild peachy flavor. "You know my favorite way to spend evenings, Lacy—with you. With or without the flowers."

"And what about nights?" She gave him a teasing grin.

He bent to trace her earlobe with his tongue and whispered, "I love spending nights with you. Have you ever heard of a night blooming jasmine?"

"That's an awful joke!" She leaned her head back and laughed aloud.

"It's late," he agreed with a lopsided grin. "Anyway, I don't have a large repertoire of flower jokes. But you must admit, that one got a smile."

"You always make me smile, Holt." She lowered her voice. "If Alita is with Mrs. Carson, why don't you stay tonight?"

"I thought you'd never ask." He kissed her throat and worked his way around her chin to her lips, continuing to lure her with his gentle passion. "After I made the arrangement for my daughter, I would have been terribly disappointed to have to spend the night alone."

"Me, too." Lacy opened her lips to another welcome kiss, this one more intense and fervent. He always managed, with ease, to pull her into his irresistible emotion. His tongue slid between her lips and teeth, taking her breath with its rhythmic plunging. She relished the taste of him as his tongue rubbed against hers.

Suddenly she craved him ravenously as a cascade of longing flooded her being. In his arms, she blossomed with him, sharing the rush of desire and wanting him as he obviously wanted her.

"Come with me," she murmured, slipping from his embrace and leading the way into her bedroom.

Eagerly, he followed her. She walked to the window and stood for a moment with her back to him as she gazed outside. Her shoulders, usually squared for action, seemed to sag beneath her blouse. The shape of her slender hips and long legs were hidden beneath the soft pleats of her skirt. She braced one hand on the windowsill and slipped out of her shoes. Standing there in her stocking feet, she was a real woman, vulnerable and unsure.

Holt was touched. He wanted to replenish her strength and confidence. He wanted to give her love, to convince her of his deep and growing affection, to cherish her. If she would let him.

"Lacy?"

She turned slowly, and in the pale gleam created by the streetlight, she looked like a silver-gilded doll. Wisps of feathery red hair drifted from the sophisticated twist she'd worn tonight. Her blue eyes were large and dark. Her smile was faint, almost mysterious.

"The moon's full," she said softly. "It's a night for activity. They say plants grow more bountifully during the full moon."

"A good night for us, Lacy? For making love?"

"Yes, I think so."

His gaze dropped to where she was unbuttoning her blouse. It gaped open enough for him to see the alluring cleavage between her pert breasts. He ached to see more as she shrugged and let the blouse slide to the floor. His breathing grew shallow as she unsnapped the front clasp of her bra and let it fall, too.

Her breasts were like alabaster. Their paleness caught the moonlight, and Holt couldn't take his eyes off them. He wanted to run his hands over their smoothness, to bury his face in their softness, to devour her. He knew that he was incapable of resisting her feminine invitation much longer. But she was in no hurry. This was her moment of glory, her seduction. And as she proceeded to undress slowly, all consciousness of their daily arguments and the problems they faced in the future fell away.

In that private, moonlit moment, they became simply two people, man and woman, who wanted and needed each other. He desired her as he'd craved no other woman.

And yet, his feelings for her ran beyond sex. If she closed her bedroom door to him right now, he'd still be back tomorrow. And tomorrow. And tomorrow. Because he didn't want to be without her. Ever.

"Lacy. I want to tell you how I feel."

"Sexy, I hope." She let her skirt slither to the floor.

"I'm only human."

She stepped out of her panty hose and panties. "Tell me more. About how you feel."

"Well, I, uh, this is quite a show, Lacy." He stared at her as she stood naked before him, a little teasing smile on her lips. He felt a band of perspiration at his neck.

She propped her hands on her hips, and the movement lifted her breasts ever so slightly. "Go on."

"I...well, I can't deny what's obvious right now." He took a deep breath and privately acknowledged the burgeoning in his groin that made normal thought—and speech—almost impossible. "But, uh, what I'm talking about are deeper feelings. Of a man for a woman, of me for you. Lacy, you must know I—"

She stepped forward and her nude body brushed his hands lightly. Unable to resist, he reached out and rested his palms on her ribs. Her skin was smooth and warm, and he was unable to think beyond the feel of her body. Her fervent kiss hushed his little speech.

Finally, she murmured against his lips. "Holt, just love me. Don't make any rash statements."

He found his breathing labored. "They aren't rash, darling. I know my head . . . and my heart."

She touched the front of his shirt, letting her fingers slide between the buttons. "Did you know your heart was pounding?"

"I don't doubt it."

"Feels like you're excited."

"Undoubtedly," he mumbled.

"I like to feel your heart close to mine." She removed his tie. "Without all this." Her hands tugged on his clothes. "Without anything in the way."

Lacy unbuttoned his shirt, kissing strategic parts of his chest along the way to discarding the garment. When he stood bare chested, she ran her hands over the muscled surface, then around to his back. Lacy loved the way he quivered when she touched him, the way his muscles tightened beneath her fingertips.

With one goal in mind, she tackled his belt and zipper, and when they were undone, she pushed the slacks off his hips. Holt took over at that point, and in another few moments, he had eliminated the clothes that kept her from him. He stood boldly before her in the filtered light, his masculine body completely aroused and eager for her.

She touched him everywhere, her hands traveling lightly, enticingly over his entire body. She caressed his tight buttocks and kissed the dark hair that trailed his stomach. Lacy enjoyed the moments of possession, of knowing that Holt was hers, knowing that she could rule the night.

He endured the sweet torture as long as he could before taking hold of her. His large hands encompassed both breasts. They were every bit as silky and soft as he'd imagined. They were as taut and graceful as he remembered. He lifted them to his lips and kissed one, then the other. He laved her nipples with his tongue and circled the pale globes with kisses.

"Lacy, you're so beautiful. I see you . . . and I want you. Now more than ever." He reached up with one hand and released the clasp that held her hair in its fancy upsweep. Instantly tousled red curls tumbled around her bare shoulders, framing her radiant face, tempting him further. She was no longer the mayor in charge of a busy political affair. She was his woman.

She smiled, an ethereal sort of smile. "I want you, Holt. I want to please you." She braced both hands on his hips and writhed erotically against him. "Want you to please me."

"How?"

"Touch me. . . ."

His hands couldn't stop touching.

"Kiss me. . . ."

His lips placed moist kisses everywhere.

"Love me, Holt. . . ."

Holt buried his hands in her hair and brought his lips down to hers, caressing them with soft kisses. His words were mere whispers in the night, but the feelings they expressed were profound to him. "I do, Lacy. Oh God, I do. . . ." His kiss became a fervent, powerful testament to his words as he swept her up in his arms.

Lacy clung to his taut male body as her feet left the floor. He was magnificent, and she marveled at his ability to keep the kiss intact as he moved across the floor.

Stumbling in the dark, unfamiliar room, he made his way to her bed, halting abruptly when his shin hit the side of the bed. They tumbled clumsily onto the mattress, losing the kiss, clutching at each other, arms and legs tangled, laughing aloud.

"You're wonderful!" she said with a gasp. "Nothing is too serious! I love loving you!"

"I'm serious about this, Lacy," he murmured, kissing her earlobe as he gathered her in his arms again. "You're very special to me. I want our intimate time together to be like paradise, not a slapstick comedy routine."

She raised up on her elbow and looked at him in the misty light. "Don't you know that's what I like so much about our relationship, Holt? You take me away from the serious aspects of life. Everything with you is fun, even making love. You've made sex exciting for me again."

"It's the way it should be."

"I agree." She bent to kiss his chest and felt his muscles tighten and quiver as she moved lower. "Do you like this? And this . . . ?" She paused to check his reaction, then continued boldly.

"I like it so much," he muttered hoarsely, "that I don't know how long I'll have control."

"Is that a threat?" she asked teasingly.

"A warning." He shifted and rolled her onto her back.

"You don't scare me with your warnings," she boasted, and arched her back as he scattered kisses from one breast to the other. His lips created a wealth of passion within her that brought her senses right to the brink of endurance.

When he touched her with his skillful, knowing hands, she writhed in sweet pleasure, delighting in the strong, sensual feelings that coursed through her entire body. Every feeling she'd ever had seemed to culminate in a tight knot in the center of her femininity. The urges were stronger than she'd ever known.

"You make me feel so good ... so alive ... like I've never felt before, Holt."

He stroked her breasts. "Sometimes just looking at you does it to me. I feel that I have to have you. And I want you urgently. But now, when I have you in my arms, I want this time we have together to last forever." His hand glided over her tummy to the soft warmth between her legs.

She quivered in anticipation as he touched her. "Me, too. Forever. Please Holt ... don't wait forever."

His large body stretched over hers, pairing his strength to her softness, his craving to her hunger. His lips covered hers, his legs stretched along the inside of hers, pushing them farther apart. He rocked forward, driving into her with a slow, sure stroke.

With a little gasp at his abundance, she received him. Her heart pounded against his; her breasts were crushed by his chest. And yet, she still pressed him closer. Their bodies molded, then combined as if they were one. She sighed in complete contentment as his passion flourished within her. She felt vibrant and went eagerly with the erotic flow that rushed through her, moving in his rhythm, feeling the heat growing in intensity.

How could she ever have doubted that he was right for her? They blossomed in perfect unison, feeling the same passion, wanting each other with the same intensity. They were perfect together, and she felt complete with him.

Suddenly, his vigor increased, his motion quickened and, with several low groans of pent-up passion, he exploded into her. Following his lead, she moved furiously beneath him, creating her own fury until she joined him in the exultation. Then they held each other close for a long while, neither wanting to let go. And that's the way she wanted them to be. Close. Close together all the night . . . all the time.

Holt was warmth and security and love. She felt the harmony they emitted and reveled in it. She knew that sometime in the night, they would make love again, but for now she curled into his arms and slept, contented and sated.

Lacy woke in the morning, never having felt so loved, so alluring, so happy. She looked around the room. Holt's clothes were gone. He'd probably slipped home before daylight to protect her reputation. Dammit, why did things have to be that way? She turned over, knotting the covers in her fists and pulling them tightly to her chin. Then she spotted a note on her dresser. Immediately she hopped up and grabbed it.

Lacy, my love

It was from Holt! Her hands shook as if she hadn't seen him in months, instead of hours.

Last night was fabulous. You are my Feast of Flowers! Tomorrow is a new day, though. Forget feelings. You must look at your responsibilities and do what's best for Silverton. Don't lose sight of the goals you and the town have worked so hard for. We'll manage our love.

Holt

Tears filled her eyes. *Forget feelings?* He was so damned logical, he'd give up his job and everything for the good of the town. But Lacy couldn't stand it. Her feelings for him were getting in the way, coloring the way she looked at everything. She bit her bottom lip. The reason was clear. Yet she didn't want to admit she'd let it happen.

She glanced back at the note. He'd used the word *love*. Did he mean he loved her? She hoped not. It would complicate the matter even more.

That was ridiculous! Why would she hope such a thing? Trouble was, she didn't know what to do about their love. So, she tried to ignore her feelings and stay in control.

She just couldn't let this happen. She had to stay in charge of the situation and not listen to her heart. It would be disastrous for them both. She'd already had that experience once. She couldn't stand it again.

But what about the Albuquerque banker's offer? It was a political move, generosity coupled with business, done all the time. Holt knew it. But she rebelled against the ethics of it. That wasn't the way she functioned.

And yet, Lacy knew, and so did Holt, that Silverton desperately needed the money that Thomas Coy could generate. Federal grants wouldn't do it all. They had to have private investments. That was part of her strategy to help Silverton along. That's why she had hosted the dinner, to alert others to their plight and how they were aiming to fix it.

She couldn't believe that in spite of their relationship, Holt was willing to sacrifice his job. But she couldn't do that to the man she loved.

10

"SO MAN, what's the big deal going down at the courthouse tomorrow?" Roman faced Holt with both thumbs hooked in his jeans pockets and a squared lift to his chin. "And how come nobody tells us what's happening?"

Holt reached into the portable chest cooler and handed Roman a canned drink. He chuckled at the boy's tough attitude. "Who told you about the council meeting?"

"I've got my ways and means." Roman held the can to one side and popped the top. It spewed with a hiss.

"I see." Holt figured the information source was probably Steve, who could have overheard Sandy discussing the situation. Roman was a wily kid, typical of a survivor, so it wasn't surprising that he would find out.

It had been two weeks since Lacy's Feast of Flowers and the disturbing offer from Thomas Coy. The proposal had caused quite a stir in town as word of the possible influx of big bucks spread. Most folks wanted that part of the deal.

But they didn't fully understand the strings Coy attached to his arrangement, namely, his son's construction company doing the work. If that happened, there was the risk of the townsfolk losing control of the direction of the projects. And clearly, Holt would move on because there would be no place for him in Coy's organization. Lacy had called the town council into a special session this Saturday so that all members and citizens, even those who worked out of town, could attend and hear both sides.

"Frankly Roman," Holt explained patiently, "I didn't think it concerned you. It's my problem."

"Hey, man, if it affects you, it affects me, and I'm concerned."

Holt suddenly felt as if he were talking with a colleague, a real friend, not a troubled kid who needed direction. "Okay, I didn't want to get you stirred up over nothing."

Roman jerked a thumb toward his own chest. "Man, I'm stirred up, all right. We start cleaning this place up, working for you, gettin' used to the way you want things done and—bingo!—they pull a switcheroo on us."

Tony and Candy joined them for a break and echoed their agreement with Roman's last statement. Holt handed each of them a soda, then took one for himself. Holt usually called a brief recess after they'd worked for an hour or so. It was a chance to share a cool drink and talk with the kids at the same time.

"First of all, you're not working just for me," Holt countered, thinking this was a good time for a little adult advice. "You're employed by the city of Silverton, just as I am. But you must realize that you're really working for yourselves, to improve your present situations and your future lives. Most importantly, you're learning a craft that you can carry with you throughout life. Nobody can take that away from you, no matter where you go."

"I'm not going anywhere, man. It's *you* I want to know about."

Today the little group had been unusually quiet while they worked. There was none of their normal chatter, none of the typical bantering and teasing among them. Now Holt understood why. They were concerned with some adult issues that could very well affect them, no matter how much he hoped otherwise.

Through Roman's source, they'd heard that the mayor had called a special meeting of the city council to consider Mr. Coy's considerable financial offer... and the strings attached. Those strings tangled the lives of others, specifically those in this room. Roman, Tony and Candy would be affected. Holt could only hope they wouldn't lose their jobs. But Holt knew that if Coy was allowed in, he would be out.

"So tell us," Roman commanded.

Holt sat on the top of the cooler and looked at the kids honestly. "You all probably know as much about this as I do. A very wealthy man from Albuquerque has offered to arrange for a lot of money to go toward refurbishing the historic district. It could mean some very good things happening to Silverton. And quicker than anyone had ever anticipated."

"It's more than that."

"Yes, Roman. It is." Holt took a deep breath. "The man wants his son to have this job."

"Your job?"

Holt nodded. "Right. My job. You have to understand, I'm just one person in the whole scheme. The town needs his financial help. And there are a lot of people around here who'll suffer if Silverton doesn't survive. Including you all." Holt motioned toward them. "And the total, the whole town, is more important than just one man."

"Can't you both work here and get it done faster?" Tony asked logically.

Holt shook his head. "There isn't room. Not enough money. And—"

"And, he wouldn't be the boss anymore," Candy explained. "Holt couldn't let someone step in and take over, could you?"

"You're very perceptive, Candy. She's right," he said to the boys. "That's the whole point. The other man, Mr. Coy's son, would be in charge of the construction. And I'd simply move on and get another job somewhere else."

"Hey, they can't do that!" Tony said.

"See, I told you this was big." Roman gestured to his friends.

"Now, listen to me," Holt said quickly. "This is what I want you all to understand." He gave them a stern look. "I can work anywhere because of what I know. I have skills and a craft that go with me, because they're in my head and my hands. No one can take that knowledge away from me. And that's what I want you to have. Knowledge and skills that no one can take from you. It's important."

"No lectures right now, okay man?" Roman shifted one hip, making his streetwise attitude obvious in his body language. "What we're thinking about today is you. This money deal isn't fair."

"Sometimes life isn't fair, Roman," Holt said. "Surely you, of all people, know that."

"Yeah, I sure do. And part of the problem is sitting around, letting things happen to you instead of taking charge."

Holt grinned proudly. "I think you *have* been listening to me a little, Roman."

"You mean you could really lose your job over this, Holt?" Tony asked.

Candy added, "And we could lose ours?"

"No, no, no. Your jobs are secure here. The mayor will see to that," Holt said with confidence, hoping he was right.

"Then we would just lose you." Candy gazed solemnly at him.

"You would have a different boss, that's all."

Roman muttered a few curses and paced the empty adobe room. "This is all about money, isn't it?"

Holt watched the reactions of his little work crew. He felt that he had to be careful with the intricacies of this political situation or they'd lose confidence in the governing system. "You have to consider this from the town council's angle. They must go with what's best for the town and what benefits the majority."

"But you *are* the best," Candy objected.

Holt grinned at her. "That's your opinion. I'm not offering the town a sizable financial contribution that will renovate several buildings and get businesses going sooner. Mr. Coy is."

"Maybe not, but you're the best man for the job," she insisted.

"It's good to know you're on my side. And I want you to know that I do appreciate it, more than you could guess." Holt stood and finished his soda. "Right now, as long as I have a job, I'd better get back to work. You, too. We have another forty-five minutes to go, and we've killed enough time. You don't want me to have to dock your pay this week, do you? Then get busy." He walked away feeling grateful for the kids' loyalty. But he couldn't help feeling beaten by the system he so vocally endorsed.

The three youths stood motionless and watched Holt disappear into another part of the adobe building. They were silent for a minute.

"Isn't there anything we can do?" Candy asked at last.

"Yeah," Roman said with a surly growl to his voice. "Yeah, there sure is. We go down fighting the system, that's what we do."

"How?" Tony looked to Roman for leadership. So did Candy.

"Okay, I'll tell ya'. The council meets Saturday morning, right? This is what we're gonna do...."

"You want to do *what*, Mrs. Carson?" Lacy stared across her desk at her sweet-faced neighbor. Her surprise was difficult to hide.

"I want to open a day-care business in my home. Sandy says there might be a grant that'll provide a low-interest loan for start-up businesses in towns like ours. And that you can help me. So, I want to sign up." She smiled and her face crinkled gently.

"Aren't you busy enough with Alita?"

"You know, Lacy, I have enjoyed looking after Alita Henderson tremendously. I'm very grateful to you for suggesting me for the job." She sighed. "That little girl has added so much pleasure to my life that I decided I wouldn't mind having more kids around."

"What prompted your idea for a day-care business, Mrs. Carson?"

"Well, you started it with your Get Busy with a Business campaign. After reading about women my age going into business, I decided I could do that, too. Everywhere there seems to be day-care shortages, and that's something I can do. My house is big and empty. And I still have a lot to offer others."

"Of course you do."

"Plus, I guess I'm a little lonely. Sandy's busy with her life and doesn't need me so much anymore. But Alita needs me. And she showed me there are plenty of other kids who do, too, like her little friend Hanna. Do you know that we don't even have a licensed day-care center in this town?"

"You've done your homework." Lacy tapped her finger on her cheek, pleased that Mrs. Carson had picked up on one of the town's deficiencies and a way she could provide a solution. "I guess we could use a day-care center."

"As jobs increase and more folks with little kids move into town, we will," Mrs. Carson stated with a businesslike nod of her gray head. "Anyway, I see all of you women so ambitious and enjoying your contributions toward fixing up this old town, I want to be a part of that, too. I want to get a piece of the action, as you young folks say." She chuckled and clutched her purse in her lap. "So what do you think, Lacy? Can I get a loan?"

"I think it's a great idea, Mrs. Carson. Actually this is a good time to apply for small-business loans in depressed areas like ours. Maybe we could label this a priority case and bypass some of the red tape. That way you could have money as soon as a couple of months, if approved."

"Well, then, I'd better get myself organized for business. I'm thinking about renovating the front rooms and having the back for my living quarters."

"Sounds as if you've really thought about this."

"Oh, a little."

Lacy walked around her desk and hugged the older lady. "I'm impressed with your initiative."

Mrs. Carson's eyes twinkled. "Well, my dear, we all are impressed with you and your initiatives. Nobody could have done as good a job at being our mayor as you, Lacy. Whoever said a lady couldn't be mayor?"

"Did anyone say that?"

"Not anymore. They've eaten their words repeatedly, with your every success!"

"Thanks for the vote of confidence, Mrs. Carson." There were times when Lacy needed that kind of encouragement more than others. This was one of those times.

Tomorrow she would be conducting the most important town council meeting in her limited experience. The outcome would affect Holt's life and probably the lives of all the kids working in his after-school program, as well as Alita's and even her own. And Lacy was convinced that Silverton would suffer, too, without the powerful influence and leadership of Holt Henderson.

Lacy was furious because Thomas Coy had bypassed her and contacted other council members with his magnificent-sounding financial offer. She could do nothing more than call a council meeting and bring the matter to the public so they could be fully informed and vote on the outcome.

She walked to the door with her arm around Mrs. Carson. "I'll give you a call next week when I get the loan forms ready. You'll need to sign them and give a brief description of your job plan."

"Thanks for all your help and encouragement, Lacy." Mrs. Carson halted. "Is it true that the council is having a special meeting tomorrow? One that might eliminate Holt's job?"

Lacy took a deep breath. "Yes, that's right. We're going to discuss the matter in an open forum and present it for a vote."

"Do you think that's fair, Lacy? I mean, after all he's done around here?"

"I really can't comment on it right now, Mrs. Carson."

"Well, you must have some feelings about it. After all, you and Holt—"

Lacy interrupted with a rush. "Please, Mrs. Carson. People aren't aware of our relationship, and I'd appreciate it if you'd continue to keep our secret. Anyway, I can't let my personal life interfere with what's best for the town."

"Do you mean that you'd let someone come in and assume his job—" she snapped her fingers "—just like that?"

"This is out of my hands."

"Then some other stranger could come in here and grab any of our jobs. Including mine. You'd let them take over, saying it was out of your hands?"

"No, I wouldn't. That's different. There are extenuating circumstances here."

"What's so different? You *are* the mayor, Lacy. You're in charge of this town. Or you're supposed to be. I can't believe you'd let some banker from Albuquerque come in and take over your town, just because he's got money."

"I'm not letting him take over! You don't understand the complications of this situation. I can't make this decision alone. It involves the town."

"I understand enough for an old lady." Mrs. Carson sniffed and hitched her purse on her arm. "Is that meeting open to the public?"

"Yes, of course. All the city council meetings are."

"Then I'll attend. And I'll see that a number of my friends do, too."

"Good. Now, if you'll excuse me, I have about a hundred things to do before I go home today."

Mrs. Carson nodded. Just before she slipped out the door, she paused. "Another thing, Lacy. If you think no one else knows about you and Holt, you're pretty dense. All anybody has to do is look at either one of you when the other is in the room." She closed the door quietly.

Lacy felt the sting of tears in her eyes. Her emotions were a wreck these days, especially since the Feast of Flowers. In an effort to stay busy and fight the tears, she fixed herself a soothing cup of chamomile tea.

During the past two weeks, she felt as though she'd been riding a roller coaster. She and Holt had grown closer. But her role as mayor had placed her in a position that she'd never envisioned. Responsibility versus objectivity. And she found it impossible to be objective now.

Mrs. Carson was right. She couldn't just let strangers come in and assume leadership here in Silverton. But what could she do about it? She had to allow the public vote. She'd spent half the night trying to figure out a strategy that would work in this case. Nothing short of influencing the council, which was against her moral stand, came to mind. The fact remained that she was mayor of this town, and she had to at least appear impartial. She was, after all, the people's representative. She had to follow their mandate.

What if they voted in favor of Mr. Coy and his thousands of much-needed dollars? What could she do if the good people of Silverton didn't care who renovated the historic district? Holt or anybody whose father had money. What *would* she do if Holt decided to leave? What would she do without him? She shuddered to think.

How would Silverton manage? He was their hope for the future, their "winning strategy." What was worse, he had captured her heart. And she was nearly crazy at the thought of losing him.

When she arrived home after seven that night, Lacy found an invitation printed in crayon and taped to her door.

Please come to my house for a great big surprise.
                                   Your friend,
                                   Alita.

Lacy pressed the note to her heart. Alita was such a dear, loving child, who reached out in many ways to Lacy. And Lacy was all too eager to reach out, also. Alita was like the daughter she'd never had...and never would have. Then it struck Lacy how very much she'd miss Alita, too, if Holt took her away.

A half hour later, she knocked on the door of the little house down the street where the Hendersons lived. Alita swung the door open and squealed in excitement as she grabbed Lacy's hand. "I have a great surprise, Lacy! But first, close your eyes."

Lacy glanced at Holt, who was standing back to let his daughter take over. He wore a sly smile and shrugged to indicate he wouldn't interfere. So Lacy did as she was told and let Alita lead her across the room.

There was some scrambling and strange scratching noises, and finally Alita said, "Okay. Down on your knees. Now, open your eyes so you can see my best surprise in the whole world!"

Lacy opened her eyes and blinked at a large cardboard box that had been placed before her. A brown-and-white creature with large green eyes poked its head above the top. "Oh, your kitten! How cute!"

"Meet Calico," Alita said proudly. "Calico, this is my best big friend, Lacy Donahue. She's the mayor, so you'd better be good." She giggled and lifted the kitten out of the box and placed it in Lacy's arms.

Holt watched as the two of them cooed over the kitten, petting it and watching it play. They seemed to enjoy pampering the tiny cat as much as it enjoyed the attention.

Finally, Lacy left Alita to play with her kitten and walked over to Holt. "I'm glad you finally agreed to let her have a pet. She's wanted one for so long."

"I know." He sighed. "I gave in to the pressure. Ah, every kid needs a pet, I guess. I just hope it isn't too much trouble."

"Cats are very independent. I'm sure Alita will do her share taking care of it."

"I intend for her to start immediately."

"You're a good daddy, Holt." Lacy patted his arm affectionately.

He took advantage of the moment while Alita was busy and steered Lacy into the living room. He encircled her with his big arms and proceeded to kiss her passionately. Neither of them noticed the passage of time until a small voice interrupted their quiet embrace.

"If you two are finished with the mushy stuff, it's time for Calico and me to go to bed."

"Oh. Yes, honey, it is," Holt agreed, prying himself away from Lacy.

Lacy kissed Alita good-night. "Thank you for sharing your great big surprise with me. Calico is a very nice kitty."

Alita hugged Lacy hard. "I think so, too."

Holt tucked his daughter into bed, then ambled back into the living room, where Lacy sat on the sofa, staring into the darkness out the window. Her mind and emotions were in a whirl tonight.

"This seems so natural," he said. "Tucking her into bed with you here. You've been a part of our lives since the day we moved in, Lacy."

"Alita has become an important part of my life, too." She shifted and tucked one foot under her leg. "She's a very lovable child."

"You're almost a part of the family, Lacy." He sat on the sofa beside her. "Almost."

She was silent a minute. "Holt, about tomorrow—"

"I understand your position, Lacy. You're caught in the middle."

"I feel so helpless. The whole thing suddenly blew out of my control." She slid her hand over his. "I don't know what I'll do if Coy wins this battle."

"It'll be tough-decision time." He turned his hand over to match his palm to hers. "I've been thinking of where I'd go for work."

"Don't talk like that."

"I have to be realistic. I have Alita to think about." He shifted and laid his arm on the sofa behind her head. "And you. I don't know what I'll do about us."

She shrugged. "What's to do?"

"I'll think of something." He sighed and let his arm slide down to drape her shoulders. "The kids who work for me are worried about how it'll affect them. I assured them you'd keep them working."

"Of course." She looked up at him. "Are you worried about them, too?"

"Can't help it. Their needs haven't been met yet. We've just started."

"You have quite a rapport with them, Holt."

"I spend a lot of time with them. You find out things." He sighed and leaned back, cuddling Lacy closer. "Take Candy, for instance. She's a tough little gal with three brothers. Their mother died last year, leaving Candy as the only female in the family and basically in charge of the home. She's so proud to be learning to be a plasterer."

Lacy relaxed against his chest. "I remember a few years ago when Tony Rios's father was killed in an accident at work. The whole town chipped in to help his mother. Now it seems that the public has forgotten that they still need help occasionally."

"Tony feels a lot of responsibility for a sixteen-year-old. This job gives him a skill, plus money to help his mother, and that's a real ego booster."

"And Roman?" She paused. "I still don't know much about him."

Holt nodded. "Nor do I. He's very careful not to reveal much about himself. But, you know, in spite of all of our differences, I like the guy."

She chuckled. "And he likes you, or he wouldn't hang around."

"Yeah. He likes people to think of him as a tough street dude. But I know he's vulnerable, like the rest of us."

"You're probably a father figure to him, Holt."

"Probably. Like you're a mother figure to Alita."

Lacy sat up suddenly. "No, I don't think so."

"Of course you are. You're young and pretty and do some really remarkable things. Plus you give her loving attention. I think you're her idea of what a mom should be. And you're a pretty good one, at that."

She pushed away from Holt and stood with her back to him. "Well, I haven't tried to do anything to win her over. It's just happened. I don't want to hurt her."

"You mean if we have to leave?" He stood behind her. "Sorry, Lacy. That's inevitable. We already care too much about you to just walk away with no pain. And there's Mrs. Carson, who's with her so much of the time. They, too, have a bond." His voice was low, and he placed his hands on her shoulders. "Maybe Mrs. Carson anticipated this and is starting the day care as a hedge."

Lacy turned around, somewhat surprised. "You knew about that?"

"We discussed it."

"You're amazing, Holt. You have your finger on every pulse in this town."

"Every one except the mayor's." He touched her neck with his fingertips. "And she's the only one I want." His fingers slid beneath her chin, and he lifted it so he could kiss her. "I think it's pretty obvious, the way I feel."

"Holt, don't." She placed her fingers on his lips to hush him.

"I know. Bad timing. Well, let's see what happens tomorrow. Then we'll deal with us."

With a sigh, Lacy gave herself up to his kiss. She wanted to encompass him, to fix the problem, to let things stay the same. But she knew that was a conclusion that couldn't be.

She spent a restless night alone, wishing she was in Holt's arms and that everything was going to be okay. Finally she fell asleep and dreamed of helping Holt and Alita pack all their worldly goods into a covered wagon. They were all dressed like the pioneers who'd settled the West a hundred years ago. In her dream, Lacy waved goodbye and cried as they pulled out, heading west, never to be seen again. She awoke feeling a distinct sense of sadness.

And on her cheeks were real tears.

LACY STRUGGLED to pull herself together for the Saturday morning meeting of the city council. She drove to the courthouse and was forced to park three blocks away because of the number of vehicles, mostly pickup trucks, lining the street.

That should have been a fair warning, but she wasn't fully prepared for what she encountered when she entered the room set aside for the council meeting. In a place equipped to hold fifty people comfortably, nearly two hundred citizens crowded together, filling the aisles and the back of the room. People were even seated on the floor in front of the council table.

She wormed her way through the dense group and took her seat at the center of the long table set up for the council. For a change, every member was present. She glanced over the crowd and spotted Sandy and Jay Amado in the front row along with Mrs. Carson. Seated on the aisle, principal Maxine Novak was surrounded by most of the high school teachers. A little farther back was Judge Corona and her husband. Then Lacy caught sight of Holt, standing in the rear with Alita. Her heart began to pound with anxiety. So much depended on this meeting. So much! And she could do nothing more than preside.

At precisely ten o'clock, Lacy called the assembly to order. "We're pleased to see such an enthusiastic turnout for today's meeting," she began with a smile. "This is the kind of interest and participation in the city's government that we're going to need to make our programs work.

"Now, today's discussion revolves around the proposed private donation of Mr. Thomas Coy, of Albuquerque. We have created a working fund that will allow private developers and investors to contribute toward the rebuilding of Silverton's economy. If mutually agreed upon, Mr. Coy has offered to defer his interest and profits for five years, so the participant is truly investing in Silverton's future.

"Now, Annie Clayton will start the proceeding by reading the proposal letter from Mr. Coy."

Annie cleared her throat. "The following is the main body of a letter that I and my fellow council members received last week from Mr. Coy.

"I am pleased to offer this investment toward Silverton's economic growth. Employment opportunities can flourish in the renovation of the historic district with the right kind of influence. I, personally, will see that people in Albuquerque who are seeking employment will be directed to your town. I will also provide a top-notch builder and his team to speed the renovations so that maximum results can be achieved."

She nodded to Lacy to indicate the end.

"Thanks, Annie," Lacy said. "Now, do we have any discussion on this matter?"

Jay Amado requested and received recognition for the floor. "That letter seems to be saying that Mr. Coy will invest in our town, but that he expects some additional consideration."

Someone from the audience spoke up. "What does he mean that he will provide a 'top-notch builder'? I thought we had one."

"I'll tell you what he means!" a loud voice exclaimed from the back.

All eyes turned to the speaker. Without hesitating, Roman Barros began making his way to the front, followed by two other teenage kids. He stood before the mayor, hands clasped in front in a polite gesture, and asked for recognition.

"Yes, Roman. Go ahead," Lacy said, a puzzled look on her face. Something was happening here. She could feel the air crackling and filling with excitement.

"I, er, we—" he gestured to Tony and Candy, who flanked him "—want to have a say in this proceeding."

"We're glad to see our youth participate in government." Lacy smiled at Roman. He had a strategy. These kids had discussed and planned this. It took a lot of courage to stand up in front of such a crowd and speak out. But here they were, ready and willing. Suddenly she was so proud of them she could shout. Instead, she kept her voice calm. "Please introduce yourselves to the council and to the citizens."

"I'm Roman Barros. And this is Tony Rios and Candy Hershey. We work for Mr. Henderson, the one who's going to lose his job if this Mr. Coy from Albuquerque has his way." He paused for dramatic emphasis, and a muffled protest ran through the crowd.

Candy spoke up. "You might say that we work *with* Mr. Henderson instead of *for* him. That's what he would say, anyway. He says we work for Silverton. But I wonder if the new guy who'll take over Mr. Henderson's job can teach me to be a plasterer. I'm learning a trade, thanks to Mr. Henderson."

"So am I." It was Tony's turn. "A few years ago, my pop died. It's been real hard for my mom and me to make it. But now, for the first time, I'm working a real job and bringing home a little money. It's all because of Mr. Henderson."

A hush had settled over the crowd by now.

Lacy blinked, scanning the sea of faces, looking for Holt. When she spotted him, she thought she saw surprise on his face. She looked again. No, it was utter amazement.

"I'll say this about Mr. Henderson," Roman added. "A dude like me, I don't have many friends. Some people you just can't trust. But Mr. Henderson, you can trust. He's one of . . . well, he's about the only friend I've got. As some of you know, we three got into a little trouble with the law. Mr. Henderson kept us from going to 'juvy' by putting us to work."

In the stillness of the room, Lacy forced her words past the huge lump in her throat. "Thank you, Roman and Tony and Candy."

"Wait! I'm not through." Roman stepped forward and held his hands up for quiet. "We know that it isn't much, but we're willing to give up our salaries and work on those old buildings for free if you people in Silverton will just keep Mr. Henderson on as the boss. He's a top-notch builder, too."

"The best," Candy added.

The crowd, which had been absolutely silent until now, burst into applause. Lacy's heart leaped with happiness. Now she knew how the town stood. They were behind Holt all the way. It was a tremendous relief.

To maintain control of the meeting, Lacy stood when she spoke. "We certainly wouldn't expect you to give up your salaries. But we'll take note of your devotion to Mr. Henderson. Perhaps we adults can take a lesson from your participation in today's proceedings. This is the democratic process in action. Anyone else like to comment?"

Taking courage and confidence from the teens, several others in the audience spoke up for Holt, including Mrs. Carson. It was impressive. Holt received support from all ages, from the rebellious youth to the conservative elderly.

When the vote was taken, the decision to refuse Mr. Coy's stipulation was unanimous. He could then decide what to do about the financial offer, although those present acknowledged that he would probably withdraw it. Nobody in the room seemed to care. The council also agreed that the teens' salaries should not be cut from the budget. Their work and training, the group concluded, was as important as renovating the historic district.

Lacy gaveled the meeting closed, knowing that they had reached a fair conclusion. She watched as the crowd closed around Holt and his daughter. *This is the way it should be*, she thought with great relief. The teenagers had developed their own strategy. And it had worked.

Holt was inundated. He shook hands and thanked people for their support. When Roman appeared, Holt grabbed his hand with extra energy. "You really pulled through for me, Roman. Thanks."

"Ah, it was nothing." Roman gave him a shy grin. "We didn't want a new boss. He might be worse than you."

"I'd almost guarantee it," Holt said with a chuckle.

"Anyway, you always said, 'Take control of your life. Don't sit back and let it happen.'"

"Well, you must have listened to me some of the time, anyway. I'm really proud of you." He shook hands with Candy and Tony. "All of you."

Holt felt euphoric. There was only one person with whom he wanted to share this moment—Lacy. But as the crowd cleared, he couldn't find her. She was gone. She'd left without him.

11

HE WAITED FOR HER. It was night before Lacy returned. He asked Mrs. Carson to stay with Alita, then walked down the street to her house.

When he knocked on her door, Lacy opened it. "Congratulations, Holt. You won a great victory for Silverton."

"But what about us, Lacy? Was it a victory for us?"

She shrugged and turned away.

He followed her inside. "I could say where've you been? But I don't have ties on your time, Lacy. Sometimes I wonder if I have any ties on you at all."

"I had to have some time to think."

"Did you come up with any answers?"

She shook her head. "Not the right ones."

"Lacy, we have to talk."

"There isn't anything more to say."

"You know what comes next."

"Please, don't."

"Lacy, you take care of everyone in this town. You have a 'winning strategy' for everyone's problems, including the town's. But who takes care of you?"

"I . . . I do."

"I want the job. But I want more from our relationship than this."

"There isn't any more, Holt."

"Yes, there is. There's marriage, Lacy."

Lacy was silent for a full minute. Then, two.

"Are you proposing, Holt?"

"Yes."

"No, please don't!"

"What's wrong with you? You're acting very immaturely about this."

"Acting?" She scoffed. "This is real, Holt. I'm just being realistic."

"You're running from love, Lacy. And there's no need to."

Large tears brimmed her eyes. "I'm not running from love, Holt."

"Then you admit it?"

"I can't deny it. I do care for you."

"Oh, my God! Say it! You love me!"

"I do." Her voice dropped. "I love you."

He crossed the space between them and took her in his arms. "And I love you, too, Lacy. More than I've ever loved before."

"More? How can you say that? You have a child by your first wife."

"What you and I have is deeper, more involved, more rounded. All parts of our lives are integrated. I love it that way. And I love you. Don't run from me. Please."

"I'm not running, Holt. But marriage is a little premature for us." She hoped to delay what she knew in her heart was the inevitable for someone like Holt. He was strong in his commitments. Obviously he wanted the same from her. That meant marriage. But could she? Should she? It hadn't worked before. What would convince her it would work this time?

"Why is marriage premature for us? That's the natural consequence to love."

"It doesn't have to be," she said stubbornly. "We can wait and see if it lasts."

"Lacy, we can't keep hiding our love." His gray eyes pleaded with her. "We can't continue these secret affairs, slipping from your house to mine and back again."

"Why not? It's worked so far."

"Because we have too many other involvements and obligations. You have a public image to maintain, and I have a daughter who will one day know what we're up to. I also have teens who work for me and look up to me. I need to have a settled life. I need a wife who's there to share our love and be a part of our family. Alita needs you, too. We should be showing them all what a loving relationship is all about."

Lacy squeezed her eyes shut and tried to pretend that he wasn't there, holding her to his pounding heart, kissing her lips with gentle passion. She tried to pretend that she wasn't responding to him, that she didn't respond every time he walked into the room, every time he touched her.

His kisses continued to torment her with their sweet seduction. She was captivated by his power and knew she couldn't escape, even if he wasn't holding her.

Holt was right. She was acting.

She was trying to pretend that none of this mattered. That she could contain their love and walk away from it or take it, whenever she pleased. And as she clung to him, Lacy knew that she wasn't a very good actress.

Finally she managed to wrench away. "Please, don't!"

"I love you, Lacy. Head over heels, heart pounding, sweaty palms—the works!"

She was silent for a moment. When she spoke, her voice was strange. "Love is not the issue, Holt."

"Well, what is? Your career? I won't interfere with that, I swear. If you want to be the mayor another term or run for governor or run for president of the whole country, I don't care. I'll help. You can do whatever you want. Just don't withhold your love."

She made her way to the sofa and sat down. "Career is not the issue, either. I'm sure we could work that out."

"Well, if it isn't love or career, what is it? Let's get the problem out in the open and work on it."

"It can't be solved, Holt."

"Of course it can. Anything can—"

"This is *my* unsolvable problem." She stared at him, her shoulders stiff, her chin barely quivering.

He sat beside her and took one of her cold, clammy hands between his. "When two people love each other, they talk about everything. They work it out together. If you're referring to this baby business, it isn't your problem. It's ours."

She licked her lips nervously. "I do love you, Holt. I'll admit it. I tried not to, tried to just keep my heart out of this. But I goofed." She lifted her gaze to his. "And I'm really sorry I let you get involved with me."

"I don't think that you had much to do with my part in this, Lacy. Don't take all the credit here."

"Well, I shouldn't have let it continue."

"Why not?"

"Because I knew all along that I couldn't marry."

"You mean that you *wouldn't* marry."

"I just can't." She took a shaky breath. "I can't go through the baby business again. And I won't put you through it, either."

"Don't tell me that because you can't have kids you won't marry me!" He halted and gazed in frustration at the ceiling. "Lacy, this is not about babies, it's about us."

"Holt, I can't have your child. Ever. I've been through the tests. Hundreds of them. I'm barren. Do you really understand what that means?"

He moved closer to her, softening his voice. "Lacy, please believe me when I say I don't care about that."

"Oh, Holt, five years down the road, you'll think how nice it would be to have a son to carry on the Henderson name. Or you'll want a child between us. You deserve those opportunities, those children. You make such a wonderful father." Her voice caught. "And I can never make it happen with you."

"I'm leaving the namesake responsibilities to my brothers. They're doing a credible job. We already have five little Henderson males and three Henderson females to carry on the family name. Anything else on your list of objections?"

"Oh yes. I have a long list. You forget I've been through this for years. I know all the solid reasons for having children. When two people love each other, eventually they want to have a child together. It's natural, as God intended."

"You're absolutely right." He chuckled, trying to lighten the mood. "It's a strange thing, that biological urge to reproduce. I've felt it. And I've done it. I helped produce a really terrific little girl. Alita is the light of my life, and I love her dearly. But I don't have to mass produce. Once is good enough for me."

She gazed at him and two tears trailed her cheeks. "I want to have your baby. But I can't."

"I can accept that, Lacy. But can you? I think the problem here lies with you and your perception of love and marriage and kids." He wiped one tear away and kissed the other. "Have you ever thought of adoption?"

"It isn't the same."

"Are those your words or your former husband's?"

She looked chagrined. "Not the same genes. Some people don't want to raise a child with other's genes."

"Let me tell you my feelings about the differences, and they have nothing to do with genes. They have to do with kids. With an adopted baby, you don't go through months of carrying the child inside you, some of it uncomfortable and unpleasant. You don't go through the physical risk of childbirth, taking a chance on the child's condition. Having attended Alita's birth, I know that labor is painful. So is adoption. Emotionally painful. Sometimes it takes lots of money and more than nine months. But the end result of both situations is a baby, or child, who needs and gives love. That part is the same."

"You're giving a different view, Holt."

"In case you haven't noticed by now, I'm different, Lacy. Whatever did or didn't work with your former husband will be altogether different with me."

"This is a serious matter to me, Holt. It was the central cause of the termination of my marriage. We couldn't get beyond it. I'm afraid that would happen with us, too. You have all the right answers now, but what about a few years down the road? What about when you—"

He grabbed her and in his strength revealed his extreme affection for her. "I can't answer about a few years down the road. I can only tell you about right now. And I love you, more than anything. But I can't continue to play this secret game of love. We both have too many public obligations. I can't let my daughter grow up knowing the woman I love and sleep with lives up the

street. That isn't a real family. What I want, and we
need, is a family."

"Holt, I...I don't know. I made up my mind after my
disaster of a marriage not to try again."

"Well, change your mind, Lacy, because you've
found someone who loves you just the way you are. I
love *you*, Lacy Donahue, not your babies. Just you. I
want—"

The ringing of the phone startled them both.

Holt released her and walked across the room, running his hand around the back of his neck. He hadn't
realized he'd have to battle the baby issue when he
mentioned marriage.

Lacy paused before answering, trying to regain her
poise. It was too late for a social call, and she worried
that there was some emergency. Her voice sounded
strained and soft. "Hello?" She glanced at Holt. "Yes,
he's here."

Holt looked up, immediately alarmed. He wasn't
expecting a call. "Is it Mrs. Carson? Something's happened?" He hurried to her side.

Lacy shook her head. "Sounds a little like Sheriff
Meyer."

Holt grabbed the receiver. "Yes...yes.... Yes, he
does.... I don't know.... No, I didn't know that.... Oh."

Lacy listened to Holt's strange conversation with in-
creasing curiosity. What in the world could he be talking about?

"Yes, I will. I'll be right there." He hung up.

"Well?" She was practically hopping up and down in
anticipation. "What's up?"

"That was Sheriff Meyer. He has Roman Barros and
his little sister, Hanna, in custody. Roman asked him
to call me. He said that I would know what to do."

"About what? What's the problem? Why are they in the sheriff's custody? What has Roman done now?"

He gazed at her, shaking his head slowly as he recalled events and bits of conversation that confirmed the allegation. "Something he couldn't help. Roman and Hanna have no adult guardians. As minors without supervision, they're considered wards of the state."

"No aunt?"

"No aunt. Nobody. Those kids have been on their own since they arrived in Silverton last summer. How in the hell did they manage? I'm going down there. Do you want to go with me?"

"Yes, of course."

He looked sternly at her. "We'll finish this conversation later. It isn't over." He kissed her nose. "And I may as well tell you now that I won't take no for an answer."

"Holt, you're impossible." She shook her head.

"Get your coat while I call Mrs. Carson. She's probably dying of curiosity to know why the sheriff wanted me. He called my house first, and she gave him this number."

Fifteen minutes later, they entered the sheriff's office. He discussed the situation briefly with Holt and Lacy, then ushered them into a back room. Roman and his little sister sat huddled together like two lonely puppies abandoned by the roadside.

Roman stood immediately. His streetwise arrogance, usually so visible in his every move, was gone tonight. But he tried to sound cool. "Hey, man. Hope we didn't interrupt anything. If you'll just tell this dude everything's okay, we'll be outta here."

"I'm glad you called me, Roman." Holt shook the boy's hand and smiled down at Hanna. "We've talked to the sheriff, and I don't think they're going to let you go that easily. You two have been living in an abandoned house?"

"What happened to your aunt?" Lacy asked.

Roman shuffled from one foot to the other. "I don't know."

"There isn't anyone, is there?" Lacy deducted accusingly. "Never was."

Roman shook his head and gazed down to where Hanna clung to his hand.

Holt stooped to talk to her. "Hi. Remember me? You came to my house once and played with my little girl, Alita."

She nodded and rubbed her nose.

"How are you doing?"

"Okay."

"Are you hungry? Would you like some French fries and a milk shake?"

She nodded and gazed hopefully up at Roman.

Holt stood and addressed Roman. "You can't see the judge until Monday. Sheriff says you two can spend the rest of the weekend in my custody... if you won't run."

Roman's shoulders twitched. "I... we aren't going anywhere if we can stay with you, Holt."

"Okay. I trust you. Let's clear out of here and get a bite to eat. We can talk about what happened."

Although it was nearly midnight, they found a fast-food restaurant open. The four of them slid into a booth. Soon everyone had cups of steaming cocoa while Roman and Hanna devoured cheeseburgers and fries.

Holt let them eat awhile before he began. "So you lied about your aunt."

"Had to," Roman explained evenly. "We couldn't have stayed, otherwise. You wouldn't have let me alone if you'd known."

"*I* certainly wouldn't," Lacy said sternly. "How did you live? What did you eat?" She gestured toward Hanna. "How could you do this to a little child?"

He raised his chin defensively. "We lived okay on handouts. A couple of restaurants in town gave us extras regularly. Places like this throw away lots of food. And she ate a good lunch at school every weekday."

Lacy felt sick. For a minute she thought she'd burst into tears at the thought of these two going through garbage to scrounge something to eat. She recalled how Roman had taken the leftover pizza when Holt had moved in. And she remembered the times she'd eaten alone or tossed out bits of edible food, enough for a child's meal. She'd heard about kids like these, but had never imagined them living in her town.

Under the table Holt slipped his hand around hers and squeezed. He could see her anguish, and his movement said, "Take it easy."

"Let's start at the beginning." Holt took a sip of cocoa. "Where'd you come from, Roman? The truth, now."

"L.A."

"Why did you chose this town? Do you have any relatives here?"

Roman shook his head.

Hanna tugged on his sleeve, and he gave her a frown.

"Look, you two are in big trouble," Holt responded tightly when he saw their visual exchange. "It's time you started telling me the truth. Otherwise, I can't help you. I can tell you this. If we don't get something worked out, they'll have to send you right back to L.A."

Hanna tugged on Roman's sleeve again. "We don't want to go back. Tell him."

Roman tried to pull away from her. "Shut up."

"Tell him about—"

"Hanna!"

"I don't want to go back there." She laid her head on his arm.

Holt's voice was low and firm. "I can only help you if I know the truth."

Roman gazed at Holt, then Lacy, then back to Holt, with a trapped expression in his eyes. He was no longer free, and he knew it. "I'm only doing this because of her. If it was just me, I could make it. But with Hanna, she's just a little kid and needs a better life than this. I hope you understand, Holt. You've got a kid like her and—"

"Tell him, Roman," Hanna whined. "I'm sleepy. I want to go to bed."

Roman took a deep breath and blurted, "Our old man is in your prison. We came to Silverton so we could visit him every weekend. Mama's gone, and he's all we have left."

There was a moment of dead silence in the booth. It was an answer that neither Holt nor Lacy had expected.

"Well, that explains some things. And complicates others," Holt said honestly.

"Look, man, don't blame him. This wasn't his idea that we come here. We just decided that we didn't want to be in L.A. for that long without our dad."

"Besides," Hanna piped up, "he got arrested way out here, and who would come see him? Don't let them take us back."

Roman shifted uncomfortably. "I only told you because I thought you might be able to help. You could tell the judge that I've got a job and I'm learning a trade. I'm trying to do better in school."

"I don't know if that's enough," Holt said with a sigh.

"Plus," Lacy added with a proud grin, "he's politically active and takes an interest in his new community. I think we have some positive things to tell the judge, Roman."

Holt nodded. At the moment, he had no idea what to suggest as a solution, but he tried to sound as if he did. "We'll see what we can do. We'll have all day tomorrow to figure out something. Right now, let's go back to my house and catch some z's. I have a couple of sleeping bags if you kids don't mind sleeping on the floor."

"Sleeping bags?" Hanna's voice was shrill. "Goody!"

As the two kids rushed ahead and climbed into the back seat of the Jeep, Holt draped his arm around Lacy's shoulders. "How could she be so excited to sleep on the floor?"

"It'll probably be the warmest she's been in weeks." Lacy hugged her own arms. "Oh, Holt, they're just so desperate. They need so much."

"Mostly, my dear, big-hearted mayor, they need love." He chuckled and whispered. "Even Mr. Wise-Guy, Street-Smart Barros needs love."

"I can see that."

The next morning, Lacy appeared at Holt's door, a large grocery bag in her arms. "Breakfast," she said, breezing past him and heading for the kitchen.

He followed her and gestured to an open box of doughnuts on the counter. "We're already having it."

She eyed the half-full container and pulled out a carton of eggs and a gallon of milk. "Boy, am I glad I came along with some nutrition."

"We are, too. We love scrambled eggs." He inspected her empty grocery bag. "What? No zucchini? Darn, and I had my heart set on it for breakfast."

She gave him a long look and proceeded with her mission of preparing a decent breakfast for the trio of youngsters. Then they headed for the country to find a place to hike and picnic. Lacy suggested Annie's Apple Farm, where there was plenty of room for them all to roam. They could fish in her stream and maybe get some homemade apple cider to go with their lunch.

Holt had forgotten all about Annie's offer of the runt dalmatian puppy until they drove into the driveway and were greeted by Annie and two spotted dogs. The large dalmatian was obviously the mother. The little pup bounced around as if it had springs for legs. As the kids piled out of the Jeep excitedly exclaiming over the dogs, he groaned.

Lacy looked curiously at him.

"We are not taking that pup, no matter what Annie says," he muttered to Lacy.

"Oh, but he's so darling!"

"No. There's too much happening in our lives now. Anyway, we just got the cat. Absolutely not!"

"You're right, Holt," Lacy agreed. "Besides, it looks like Alita has already lost interest in the dog."

They climbed out of the Jeep and watched the girls racing for an old tire swing hanging from a tree in the front yard. Roman was the only one petting the puppy.

"This is Pepper," Annie said. "Do you like her?"

Roman straightened and shrugged. "She's okay."

Although Roman tried to pretend he didn't care for the rambunctious animal, it was obvious to the adults that the boy and the puppy had established an instant bond.

That afternoon, Holt and Lacy left Alita with Mrs. Carson while they took the Barros kids to visit their father, Manuel Barros, in the prison. Holt wanted to meet the man and evaluate the situation further.

Lacy had never been inside the prison, and it was an emotional experience for her. She observed the obvious love between the kids and their father. And she saw the almost hopeless situation of a man imprisoned and unable to fulfill the needs of his children.

That evening, after the kids were tucked into bed, Holt and Lacy sat in the kitchen with cups of steaming tea on the table between them.

"What a weekend," she said with a heavy sigh. "Parts of it were nice, parts of it were heartbreaking."

"It'll be heartbreaking if they're sent back to L.A."

"Do you think Judge Corona will do that?" Lacy folded her arms on the table and leaned forward. "They seemed to enjoy the apple farm. And, no matter what he says, Roman really liked the puppy."

"Yeah. It's too bad he can't have a dog. But his lifestyle doesn't allow it."

"They've been terrific today. It's hard to believe they have so many problems."

"The judge may not have a choice because of the laws. She probably will send them back to L.A. if they don't have a place to live and a guardian." Holt shifted back in his chair. "Roman's basically a good kid. He just has a world of troubles. He needs discipline and love, like all kids. It's Hanna who worries me the most. She's so young and impressionable."

Lacy sighed. "She's precious."

Holt glanced pointedly at Lacy. "She's somebody else's child...one with different genes. But to me, she's just a child who needs lots of love and care."

Lacy toyed with her cup. Holt was right. Hanna was a beautiful child who needed love. "When will their father be out of prison?"

"He was caught transporting stolen goods across state lines. With good time, he'll probably get out in a year and a half."

"That's not very long." Lacy gave him a hopeful look.

"Not unless you're the one spending it behind bars."

"Yeah, I guess." Lacy sipped her tea. "Do you think the kids knew when they came here that it would be over a year before their dad was free?"

Holt shrugged. "I doubt if they even gave it a second thought. They just wanted to be near him."

"But they lived with their aunt in L.A.?"

"Apparently it wasn't a good situation."

Lacy shook her head. "You have to admire them for spunk."

"I do," Holt said slowly. "And I want to do something to help them, Lacy."

"You do, Daddy?" A child's voice broke into the hushed conversation. "Oh goody! What can we do?"

Lacy and Holt looked up to see Alita standing in the doorway in a long pink nightgown. She gazed from one to the other with a tentative smile.

Lacy smiled back, thinking the child looked like an angel with big gray eyes and tousled brown hair.

Holt rose immediately and scooped her up into his arms. "Alita, what are you doing here? You should be asleep by now."

"I heard you talking about Hanna and her brother. Why can't they just stay here, like they are now?"

"We don't have room for them. They have to sleep on the floor. That isn't fair. How would you like it if I gave you a sleeping bag and said, 'Here's your bed-room, kid'?"

Alita frowned. "I wouldn't like that. But Hanna said it was better than she had all summer. They used to sleep in that place where you work, Dad."

"Where's that, honey?"

"The building you're making new again."

"The historic adobe?"

She nodded.

"Hanna told you that?" Holt looked at Lacy with a new, understanding expression.

"They were our vagrants," Lacy said softly. She shook her head. "I can't believe it."

"That's probably why they vandalized it," Holt deducted sourly. "They wanted to run us out."

"Now Roman's working there to fix it up. What a coincidence." Lacy moved toward them and kissed Alita lightly on the cheek. "G'night, sweetie."

"Will you make my dad let them stay, Lacy?"

"We'll see."

"Oh no," Alita wailed. "That means maybe not. We could put another little bed in my room for Hanna. Then we could put another bed in Daddy's room for Roman."

"Hmm," Holt mumbled, and gave Lacy a whimsical glance before whisking Alita off to bed. When he returned, Lacy was sliding into her jacket, and he held the back for her. "Out of the mouths of babes. She has a point, Lacy."

"I think the daughter is as big-hearted as her father."

"It's a good thing, because we're all in this together. You too, Lacy." He hooked one arm around her shoulders, and they walked slowly to the door. "Thanks for spending the day with us. It was sort of like a family."

"Yes, it was. And I enjoyed every minute."

"As a father, I must admit I sympathize with Manuel Barros's dilemma. I know he committed a felony, and I'm not condoning that. But I sure would hate to be away from my kid for that length of time."

"I can't believe all this is happening right here in Silverton." Lacy stopped at the door. "And I thought we were immune to certain situations because we're a small town."

"Want me to walk you home?" They stepped out onto the porch. "I'm sure the kids will be okay alone for a few minutes."

"No, thanks. You shouldn't leave them, even though this is a safe town."

"I hear this town has a humdinger of a mayor. I understand she tries to solve everyone's problems but her own."

Lacy grinned. "Did you hear she eats flowers when she's frustrated with all those problems?"

"Um-hmm. We could all use a bunch of flowers on our plates now and then. But I wonder what this problem-solver would do about loving a family man?"

"She's skeptical of another relationship, I hear."

"Or scared?"

"No." She paused. "Well, maybe a little."

"Ah, honesty! That's a step in the right direction." He turned her toward him and molded her to his lean form. "Trust me, Mayor. I love you. And I'm going to figure out a strategy to get you. Just like you did to get me. It works both ways, you know, Mayor Donahue."

"What?" She laughed.

"I'll figure out something...just give me a little time. I can't let these kids be taken back to L.A. They might never get to visit their father. And no telling what kind of life they'd have there. On the other hand, I can't lose you, Lacy. I love you too much." His kiss left no doubt.

When he finally released her, Lacy walked slowly up the street to her house. She thought of Holt's kiss and what it did to her. She thought of those kids. All three of them needed so much. And she remembered Mrs. Carson saying that she still had something to offer. Lacy wondered if she did.

Holt said they needed a strategy. She walked the floors of her big empty house half the night, trying to figure one that would work. There was only one that she could think of, and yet she hesitated. She had her own convictions. She'd been through too much. She couldn't forget the past.

Or could she?

12

LACY SIPPED lemon-mint tea and tried to get her priorities in order. It had been a busy Monday so far, made worse because she'd spent such a restless night. For once, she wanted the town to stay quiet. She had her own life to get in order.

But that wasn't to be. Silverton was like a child, demanding attention. Everything seemed to be coming to a head at once. All today.

Any other time she'd be ecstatic. It was what she'd worked for all this time. Today, though, she had to solve the immediate. She needed to concentrate on Holt and how to solve the complications in their lives.

She'd vowed not to marry again, at least for a few more years, because of her infertility. The pain she'd experienced in her first marriage had been too great to risk it again. Holt, though, made her see that problem differently. He claimed it wasn't as great as his love.

Strangely, by her involvement with him, she had become drawn into a family life of sorts. She'd experienced it in small doses with Holt and Alita during the months since he arrived. But this past weekend, she'd been immersed in an even larger family with the Barros kids. And she'd loved all of it. She had to decide if her former vow to herself was valid anymore. To Holt it didn't seem to matter. So what about her?

Lacy walked around the room. This old office in this ancient courthouse had seen a world of changes since it was built almost a century ago. It had even seen a few changes since she took office. She was proud of her innovations and of what she had done to revive the town. Today these old walls would hear another decision— one that might change her life completely.

As if that weren't enough to keep her totally preoccupied, she'd already received two long-distance telephone calls that would change Silverton's future. And affect them all.

"Lacy?"

She looked up to acknowledge her receptionist. "Yes, Roberta?"

"Mr. Henderson is here."

"Send him in." Lacy straightened her shoulders and gave Holt a brave smile. As soon as she saw him closely, her spirit softened. With dark circles framing his usually bright eyes, he looked almost as bad as she did. Obviously heavy decisions had kept him awake last night, too.

He wore his navy jacket today, the one that made his shoulders look a mile broad and usually made his eyes seem more blue than gray. The creases in his tan slacks, were razor sharp. Obviously he wanted to impress the judge when he made his appearance before the bench in an hour.

What he did right now, though, was impress the devil out of her. Lacy remembered how he'd garnered her attention and admiration in this very office almost three months ago when he was interviewed.

months...and a thousand beautiful moments ago. She took a deep breath. "Want some hot tea?"

Holt's gaze engulfed her, the way he wanted to physically engulf her. But he couldn't...didn't. She was large eyed, and her skin looked especially pale today. She appeared almost delicate. Her red hair was tousled more than usual. She wore a salmon-colored sweater with brown slacks, and she looked fantastic. He wanted to sweep her into his arms and away from everything and everyone. But he couldn't.

Neither of them could leave. They had responsibilities. That was where his strategy came into play. If it worked, everybody would win. If not, they'd all lose.

Roman and Hanna needed the positive role model she could offer. Alita needed a mommy. But if Lacy refused his love, he would be the biggest loser of all. And, deep inside, he knew it was a situation that might drive him from Silverton. He couldn't imagine living here without having her close.

"No, thanks," he said as he took a few more steps into the room. "Lacy, we need to talk."

"Yes. I have some good news."

"Oh?" He held his breath, not knowing what to expect.

"I got a call a few minutes ago." She smiled hopefully. "Your federal grant has been approved. In a few weeks we'll have enough money for you to hire a crew and finish all the historic buildings. It's a three-year program. By then, all of the structures should be in pretty good shape and maybe most of them can be occupied and earning their keep." She paused. "Three years, Holt. Isn't that great?" She meant that he'd have a job here in Silverton for three years, if he wanted it.

Normally he'd be thrilled. But today, he wasn't sure of anything past the next couple of hours. "Yes, that's great," he managed, repeating her words.

"Also, I've got Mrs. Carson's loan forms ready for her to sign. She'll be thrilled."

"That's good."

Lacy sighed with a frustrated little chuckle. "I also got another interesting call."

"It's been a busy morning."

"Very. This one was from an executive of the community college." She paused, weighing her words and her thoughts at the same time. "They have a proposal to discuss with the Economic Development Department, which is Annie. And you."

"Me?" He looked surprised. He wasn't academically prepared for teaching at the community college. Why else would they want to talk with him?

She nodded. "They want you to serve on an advisory board. I recommended you highly. I told them you'd be excellent for what they need." She should be wildly excited about the community college's proposal. So why wasn't she? Right now, she could only think about how Holt fit into *her* future. Silverton, the spoiled brat who demanded attention, could take care of its own future.

"Which is?"

"They didn't give me all the particulars, but they want to discuss the possibility of turning the old copper processing plant into a trade school. It'll be a place to teach technical skills to those who've lost jobs or been placed out of the job market for whatever reason. And they want you to be a part of it. Apparently you've made an impression on them, and they see the training as a necessary first step for those who are job seeking. It could mean that Silverton would be a center for trade skills, a sort of workers' clearing house."

Holt's face became animated. "Whether I'm involved in it or not, it sounds like a great idea. I agree wholeheartedly. We have to admit that not everyone is college material. I feel that job training these days is more important than ever. This will help those who have lost their jobs as well as the young ones coming along, like Tony and Roman and Candy, who probably won't be able to go to college."

"I agree."

He paced the room, and she waited. Finally he spoke haltingly. "I think you know . . . that I want to keep Roman and Hanna until their father gets out of prison."

"I figured. And I think it's admirable. But what about the future when their father gets out of prison and wants to take them back to L.A.?"

"We discussed that and he feels, as I do, that there's more opportunity for him and his kids if he stays right here in Silverton."

Lacy shook her head and tried to think clearly. What was wrong with her? She felt lost and confused and wondered if she was losing her grip on reality. But Silverton *was* her reality.

Holt moved closer and caught a whiff of her heady, spicy fragrance mingled with the half cup of lemon tea she held. There were moments when he thought he couldn't bear to be without her another night. And there were times when he wondered if they'd ever spend another night together. "Lacy, all your innovative strategies are working. You've stuck by this town, given

it some new blood and ideas, and it's all working. Your
dreams are coming true."

"Not all of them." She shrugged and shook her head,
dazed by the overwhelming power of Holt's presence
as he stood within a hand's reach of her. "All of these
things sound fine. But they're in the future, Holt. They
haven't happened yet, and they won't happen tomorrow. We just have to hang on until then. Hoping...."

"That's what I want to talk to you about, Lacy. The
future. *Our* future."

" 'Ours'?"

"Definitely ours. You figure very prominently into
it. If you'll agree to my scheme."

"Your 'scheme'?"

"Ah, my strategy. You seem to understand strategies. You've used them—"

"Now, listen!"

He ran a finger over her top lip. "*You* listen, Mayor.
Listen to one of your most ardent admirers and sup-
porters. One of your constituents who's benefited the
most from your term in office. Without you, I'd probably still be drifting, trying to be a good father, searching for something to hold my life together. For someone
like you, Lacy...." He placed his hand loosely around
her wrist.

She shivered at his touch, wanting more, not daring. They were, after all, in a public office. She figured
her pulse, like her heart, was raging.

"Listen to my strategy, Mayor Lacy Donahue. I happen to love you. Very much. And I want Your Honor's
sweet, seductive body in my bed every night. Now, I'll
be the first to admit that we've had a few wonderful
weekends and a couple of terrific stolen nights to-

gether. But that's not enough for me." He stepped closer and slid his hand to her rib cage. "I want you with me, always and forever."

"Holt...." She felt breathless and excited and curious all at once.

"Don't interrupt. This speech is mine," he admonished gently. "The way I figure it, if we were alone on an island, our love could be declared and consummated before God and the wild creatures without bothering the nearest clergy. And I wouldn't give a hoot. But Lacy, we aren't alone. We live in an active, close-knit community, and we have obligations and responsibilities to that community. I have kids who look up to me. And you have a whole town who looks to you for guidance."

"That was a very nice speech."

"I'm not through." He took the cup of tea from her hands and set it on the desk behind her. Then he held her hands, sandwiching them between his.

She smiled. "Are you asking me to marry you?"

"No. Oh no! I've already explained, it isn't that simple." He shifted his thigh against hers. "I'm proposing a strategy, a winning one, I hope. Alita needs a mommy. She also needs another girl or two around the house to help offset the male-female ratio. Roman and Hanna need a strong role model, and I can't come up with a better one than the mayor of the town. And I need... I want a friend, a lover, a wife. I'd like to have someone by my side to keep me steady and support me in my endeavors."

"You *are* asking me to marry you!"

"But, don't you see, darling? It isn't just me you'd be marrying. It'd be all of us. It'd be a commitment, bigger than the two of us. We all have jobs to do, goals to reach, achievements to accomplish. And I'll try to understand if you want to hold off and go it alone with yours.

"If you refuse because you can't have a baby. . ." He shrugged. "I'll accept it. I won't really understand, though, because if you still want a baby after all this, I don't know where we'd fit it in. But we'd try."

"Sounds like your home would be a wild place with all that going on."

"I'm afraid so." His arms slid around her back, and he spread his hands on either side of her spine. "We'd have to squeeze in time for us."

"Sounds like you need a bigger house."

"Could be."

"Why don't you use mine? It's way too big for one woman and her cat. I don't know why I ever bought one so big."

He grinned. "Maybe it was a part of your strategy."

"What's that?"

"Buy a big house and maybe enough people will come along to fill it." He kissed her lips in a quick, sure motion. "And we did. Was that a yes?"

"Was that a proposal?"

"I'll say yes if you will."

She laughed—nervously, generously, happily. "Yes! Yes! Yes!"

He picked her up and whirled her around the old office. "I love you so much, Lacy Donahue, I can't stand it. I want to love you until . . ." His words were muffled and hushed by her all-consuming kiss. And in the quiet interim, the old walls of the ancient courthouse absorbed even more loving, beautiful memories. . . .

LATER THAT MORNING, Holt and Lacy stood before the judge, flushed, nervously exchanging glances and tight smiles. Roman wore a new shirt, and it took Lacy a minute to recognize it as one of Holt's. Hanna's braids were decorated with a bright red bow at the end of each one. Someone had braided her hair neatly. She wondered if Holt had done it. She hid a smile imagining Holt and Roman hovering clumsily over the little girl's hairdo.

The sheriff's deputy presented a folder of papers explaining the Barros children's case, and the mood became somber. Judge Corona studied the papers through wire-rimmed glasses, then lowered them to scrutinize the group. "These kids have been with you since Saturday night, Mr. Henderson?"

"Yes, Your Honor."

"Any problems with them?"

"No ma'am. Not a bit. I've known them for some time, and we get along well. We have a good rapport." Holt cleared his throat. "But there's more to their situation than what's in the report you're reading."

Judge Corona turned the corners of her mouth downward. "Oh yes? What?"

"Manuel Barros, their father, is in the federal prison here. He's serving one to five years for transporting stolen goods across state lines. The reason Roman and Hanna came to Silverton in the first place was to be able to see their dad occasionally."

"Well, well, well, this is new information, indeed." The judge folded her arms and leaned forward on the desk. "During this time, they've been living in an empty house. No supervision whatsoever?" Her gaze went from Roman to Hanna. "This little girl has been living like a homeless waif?"

"No, ma'am." Roman took the defensive. "I took good care of her. She ate three squares a day and had a roof over her head."

"And just what did you plan on doing to keep her warm later this winter?"

"Well, I, uh, hadn't planned that far ahead. But I'd have found her someplace warm."

"I have a suggestion, Your Honor," Holt said, stepping forward to drape his arm around Roman's shoulders. "These children have no real home. Back in L.A. they were living with an elderly aunt. Actually, if we can arrange it, they're better off staying here in New Mexico so they can retain some relationship with their only living parent, their father. I've met the man, and he does care for his children. Obviously they care for him."

"Yes, so what's your suggestion, Mr. Henderson?"

"I'd like to keep them in my home until their father can take over as he should. With good time, he'll be getting out of prison in another year and a half, at the most. I know these kids. I care what happens to them. Roman has worked for me after school for about a month. And I have a little girl around Hanna's age. They'll do fine together."

"Foster care, eh?" Judge Corona leaned back and evaluated the situation. "That'll require a social worker to investigate your home, Mr. Henderson. But I can tell you right now, the fact that you don't have a wife won't set well with the state agency."

Lacy stepped forward. "But he'll have a wife. As soon as possible."

Judge Corona lifted her head and glared. "Lacy? You?"

"Yes, Your Honor. Me," she said proudly, and slipped her hand into Holt's.

Every eye in the small courtroom turned to them. And the low chattering hushed to silence.

"Why, Lacy, this is quite a surprise," the judge said.

"I know. But I like to keep the town on its toes."

"Well, I'd say you've just knocked us back on our heels. First these kids, then a sudden marriage. Are you sure?"

She smiled up at Holt. "Very sure. Never more sure about anything in my life."

"Yo, man, what a scene!" Roman said excitedly. "We just got ourselves a family."

"And I just got myself a bunch of kids," she said laughingly to Holt. Then she looked up at him seriously. "When do you want to make this all legal and proper?"

"Just like you said, Lacy. As soon as possible."

She smiled at him, her devious mind concocting another scheme, this one the wildest yet. Lacy turned to the judge. "Vinna, do you have the legal power to marry someone?"

"Well, it's not the usual sort of thing a juvenile judge does, but . . . of course, I do have that vested power."

"Great! Could you meet us this afternoon in my office? And bring along whatever papers you need to make a marriage official and legal. We'll provide the witnesses. And don't worry about the text. We'll provide the words of commitment."

Holt blinked and looked down at her. Was this happening, really happening? Was it happening now?

Would he have a wife and an extended family before sundown?

"You aren't backing out now, are you?" she dared. "If you're worried about what to say, I'll help you with that."

"Not on your life, my honorable mayor!" He wrapped his arm around her shoulders. "I can think of my own words of commitment, thank you."

Holt relented and allowed Roman and Hanna to remain out of school for the day. And he retrieved Alita from her school so she could be a part of the most important day of his life, a day that would change all their lives.

Lacy raced home and changed into something more appropriate for a wedding. She chose a pale blue suit that matched the blue in her eyes and tried not to dwell on the unnerving fact that this was *her* wedding. She grabbed a handful of blue star-shaped love-in-a-mist and chamomile flowers and some green sprigs of lemon verbena and rosemary and tied them with a ribbon for an herbal bouquet.

When she returned to her office, she was amazed to find the room crowded to overflowing with friends, colleagues and townsfolk who wanted to witness the mayor's most unusual event to date. Her marriage.

Holt's head towered above them all, and she sighed with relief and made her way toward him. He swept his arm protectively around her and pulled her close. "Ready to make this official, Your Honor?"

She took a deep breath and released it. "Ready. Oh yes, very ready. And you?"

He placed his hand over his heart. "Got my words of commitment right here."

"Me, too."

They faced the judge eagerly. . . .

THE HONEYMOON took place in Cloudcroft the next weekend. Mrs. Carson agreed to watch Alita and Hanna. Sandy and Jay Amado took Roman, who was glad to be with his pal, Steve. Child care for the newly formed Henderson family was a team effort, but then, so was everything connected to the success of Silverton.

"Is this real?" Lacy asked as she stood at the window of their hotel room.

"We are. Our love is. The rest is conglomeration."

"I still can't believe it."

"How can I convince you?" Holt approached her back, placing his hands on her bare arms. She wore a filmy, pale blue nightgown that hung from spaghetti straps and draped her body with a fantasylike aura.

They stood together, sharing the majestic view of snow-crested mountain peaks that surrounded their little Cloudcroft love nest. The Sunday morning air was filled with the swell of church bells.

"Do you wish you'd had a church wedding?"

"Not at all." There was no hesitation in her response. "We declared our love before God and everybody. What more could we need?" She patted one of his hands. "This is like a scene from *The Sound of Music*," she murmured softly. "So beautiful."

"They had more kids than we do."

Lacy chuckled and laid her head back on his bare shoulder. Her husband was so strong and sexy this morning, and touching him reminded her of their arduous lovemaking this weekend. They had loved fervently and often, as if to make up for the lack of privacy they knew awaited them when they returned home that night.

"You know, Holt, in all my agony over not being able to have a child, I never thought much beyond the baby stage. I was stuck on the notion that an infant would make me happy. Now, though, I've skipped babyhood altogether and have jumped into the lives of real kids. Already Alita has asked if we can get Hanna a different kitten so they won't have to share Calico and wear her out."

"She put you up to asking me? How do you feel about getting another one?"

"I don't mind, if they'll help with the care and feeding. Actually, if you have one kitten, what's two?"

"Next thing we'll hear is Roman—"

"Annie already approached me. Roman did take to that puppy the minute he saw it."

"And?"

"I didn't make any promises until I could talk with you."

"A puppy is much more trouble."

"It might keep Roman busy training him."

"Might."

"Every boy needs a dog, Holt."

"What do you know about every boy?"

"So they say. Those who know about kids."

"Hmm, a new cat, a new dog and daily nutrition. You're going to be a fine mommy." He wrapped his arms tighter around her, enfolding her with his masculine strength.

"I hope I can give them what they need."

"You have exactly what they need. Plenty of love."

She clasped her hands over his. "And do I have what you need, Holt? Sometimes love isn't enough. The first time around, it wasn't enough." She sighed with a little shudder.

"Maybe the other love wasn't strong enough. I promise that your love is enough for me, Lacy. And it's strong enough to last a lifetime." He lifted her hair and pushed it to one side so he could kiss her neck.

She turned in the circle of his arms and lifted her face to him. "I love you, too, Holt. In you I have the best, most magnificent love of all."

"I could argue with that," he said with a little smile. "Because I think I have the best in you." He nuzzled her neck beneath her earlobe and continued his trail of kisses until he reached her mouth. Then his lips covered hers with an unquenchable passion. When he lifted his head, his eyes were heavy lidded, his voice low. "We have to protect our love, Lacy."

"From whom?" she scoffed with a little chuckle.

"From the disruptions of our busy lives. From the natural but nonstop needs of our children."

"But, Holt, they're our family. They won't come between us. They'll enhance us."

"Didn't anyone ever tell you that children are demanding? Just like your precious town. Lovable, but at times, interfering."

She considered his evaluation and remembered her feelings last Monday morning when she'd wanted to concentrate on her relationship with Holt and the city affairs kept intruding. She'd even thought of Silverton as a spoiled child requiring immediate attention.

At that moment, she had wished it would go away. But it hadn't. And she'd had to figure how to manage both her personal life and the public needs.

"I see what you mean," she said finally. "And I think I have a very brilliant husband to realize those things."

"I'm thinking of us and how important it is for us to protect our love and keep it alive. And thriving."

"Like now?" She nestled in the erotic comfort of his strong, engulfing body. "You seem to be thriving now." She grinned knowingly.

His lips sought hers in a long, lingering kiss. "Ah yes, Lacy. Having you so close and dressed like a fairy queen in this filmy gown keeps me viable." He rocked his hips forward, thrusting his arousal against her.

She slid her hand between them and touched him intimately and quite boldly. "Very viable, I'd say."

"Shall we work at keeping our love alive . . . right now?" His tender kisses circled her throat like a moist necklace.

She lolled her head back to partake in and enjoy every delightful nibble. "I wouldn't want to stand in love's way."

He gently pushed aside the thin straps of her nightgown and kissed each shoulder. "Mrs. Henderson, you have made me the happiest man in the world with your love." And he meant it. Filled with passion for the lovely redheaded mayor of Silverton, he scooped her up in his arms.

Lacy draped her arms around his shoulders and kissed his neck. "Thank you for showing me that I have enough love to go around. And that I don't have to prove my love, just show it."

They spent the next hour—and the rest of their lives—happily showing their love.

THE FIRST TEMPTATION
OF MAGGIE DAVIS...

Reviewers and readers alike describe her books as "steamy", "sizzling", "hot".... And now she's writing for Harlequin!

Watch for *Dreamboat*, an irresistible Temptation in October.

Available where Harlequin books are sold.

JAYNE ANN KRENTZ
WINS HARLEQUIN'S
AWARD OF EXCELLENCE

With her October Temptation, *Lady's Choice*, Jayne
Ann Krentz marks more than a decade in romance
publishing. We thought it was about time she got our
official seal of approval—the Harlequin Award of
Excellence.

Since she began writing for Temptation in 1984, Ms
Krentz's novels have been a hallmark of this lively, sexy
series—and a benchmark for all writers in the genre.
Lady's Choice, her eighteenth Temptation, is as stirring
as her first, thanks to a tough and sexy hero, and a
heroine who is tough when she has to be, tender when
she chooses....

The winner of numerous booksellers' awards, Ms Krentz
has also consistently ranked as a bestseller with readers,
on both romance and mass market lists. *Lady's Choice*
will do it for her again!

This lady is *Harlequin's* choice in October.

Available where Harlequin books are sold.   AE-LC-1

The series that started
it all has a fresh new look!

The tender stories you've always loved now feature a
brand-new cover you'll be sure to notice. Each title in
the Harlequin Romance series will sweep you away to
romantic places and delight you with the special allure
and magic of love.

Look for our new cover wherever you buy
Harlequin books.

Have You Ever Wondered If You Could Write A Harlequin Novel?

Here's great news—Harlequin is offering a series of cassette tapes to help you do just that. Written by Harlequin editors, these tapes give practical advice on how to make your characters—and your story—come alive. There's a tape for each contemporary romance series Harlequin publishes.

Mail order only

All sales final

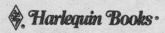